I0684359

The Land of Heaven

Yvette Shoshanah
Cherith Brook

Land of Heaven Publishers
Madison, Wisconsin

The Land of Heaven
(Revised)

Written by Yvette Shoshanah and Cherith Brook
Published by:
Land of Heaven Publishers

Library of Congress Catalog Card Number 97-74595
ISBN 9780965910651

**Dedicated to
the Father, Son and Holy Spirit
Who inspired these stories**

Jesus tells us that unless we enter heaven as innocently as a child we won't enter at all. There are no antagonists or villains in the land of heaven.

Chapters
Part 1

Part 2

The Land of Heaven

Part One

Chapter 1 -- A Valentine Story

I remember so clearly my arrival in heaven. Not long after I met Jesus, a quiet breeze picked me up and I floated ever so gently over beautiful trees and flowers. It didn't seem strange to float in midair; normal had lost its meaning in this new land of heaven. I wondered where I was going, knowing it would be someplace marvelous. All of heaven was one extraordinary surprise after another. I looked down at the passing terrain and found I was coasting over the Golden Sea. I had never been on the other side of the great sea; excitement coursed through my body.

I wondered what had prompted the breeze to come and carry me away. I had been thinking about two dear friends on earth, Charity and Vicky, praying fervently that God would send them His love. Then, before I could utter a word of surprise, I'd floated away like the wisp of a cloud.

The breeze subsided and I began to descend. The ground below looked red. Had this been earth, I would have been afraid of dropping into a huge prairie fire, or a river of molten lava. But in heaven there was no fear. I was merely puzzled. As I neared the ground, I discerned many pieces to the puzzle of red prevailing over other colors. Valentine hearts of every size and shape grew on the trees and shrubs. Even the grass had tiny valentine flowers.

"How absolutely wonderful!" I gasped.

When my eyes adjusted to their brilliance, I saw that each heart was distinct from the others. I picked a small one with swinging arms and dancing feet. It twinkled and smiled at me. I kissed it gently. Straightaway it flew to earth. Then I noticed a stately heart with royal red and white lace. When I reached to pick it, it jumped from the branch into my hand. I laughed and kissed it too. It also flew to earth.

The gentle breeze returned and once again I ascended into the heights. Without a word from the Father, I knew He had answered my prayer.

Chapter 2 -- The Missing Stone

A soothing light shining through my veranda window rested softly on my face. I closed my eyes for a short nap. Lying on the window seat in the study of my heavenly home, I listened to the merry, musical voices of children at play with accompanying singing birds.

I'd never dreamed rest could be so pleasant while living on earth. I vividly recalled hating to nap as a child, always thinking I'd miss something important.

Here in heaven, I knew the Holy Spirit would wake me for any important event. Indeed, the air would become so full of God's presence and power that sleep would be impossible.

One of heaven's celebrations came to mind and my eyes opened wide with excitement. There were so many celebrations in heaven. *I shouldn't think about them now*, I thought, determined to rest.

No sooner had I closed my eyes than the sound of flapping wings gave me a start. Camelia, a bright-winged bird, flitted in and out of my window. Eventually, she lighted on my bureau.

"Camelia, dear, you'll have to visit me some other time. I have a mission to go on and I want to rest first." I turned my head and went to sleep.

Shortly after my visit to the Valentine Garden, Jesus had asked me to travel to a distant part of heaven and minister to two young girls who had recently arrived from earth. It was almost time to embark on my journey and I could barely contain my emotions.

Camelia was fascinated by the shiny, gold ribbon in my hair. She skillfully gripped it with her beak and pulled it free, then flew around the room with the ribbon waltzing after her.

"No, Camelia! Bring it back!" I spoke as kindly as I could. She didn't mean to bother me; she was only playing. She dropped the ribbon on my couch.

I was about to close my eyes again when the light in my room deepened from soft, light gold to bright gold. I sensed it was time to begin my mission. After smoothing my gown, I tied the gold ribbon in my hair. "I must take my white stone," I told myself.

Jesus had given me a white stone with my new name written on it. It was so precious to me that I took it everywhere I went. I looked on the writing table where I had left it. The table's empty top stared back at me.

It's gone! Camelia must have taken it! Poor dear, she can't resist a shiny object. She doesn't know any better. I consoled myself thinking, *Jesus will help me get it back.* Then I turned my thoughts back to my mission.

"There's so much of heaven I haven't seen yet, Father. May I travel slowly through the land and enjoy its beauty?"

His answer came through the window on a gentle breeze, "Yes, My daughter."

I had seen the Golden Sea and the Valentine Garden, but there was so much more. *Eternity won't be enough time to see it all.* Then I remembered that there is no time in heaven. I still had difficulty relating to that.

I shivered in anticipation of the places I would see. *But how can I go without my white stone?* I told myself that perhaps I would meet Jesus on the way. *What a thrill that would be!* With that thought in mind, I closed the door and stepped merrily along the flower-lined walk in front of my home.

Spotting Camelia perched on top of a small fruit tree, I asked, "Camelia, dear, do you have my white stone?" She tilted her head and looked at me perplexedly. Spotting my gold ribbon again, she flew over and teasingly pulled at it.

"I'll give you the ribbon if you'll bring back my white stone."

She danced on my head as I loosened the ribbon, then she grabbed it and disappeared into the foliage of a tree. She was so fast I had to laugh. I waited and waited for her to return. *I can't wait any longer.*

Turning to start down the path, I saw a man walking toward me. My heart beat rapidly, my mouth went dry, my eyes filled with joyful tears. I was about to experience again the most indescribably wonderful and blessed reward of heaven: Jesus, my Lord, was walking toward me. The awe and wonder I felt in His presence could never diminish with time or familiarity. Even the earliest arrivals in heaven, those He'd brought with Him from Paradise after His death on the cross, still spoke of how they unfailingly receive a fresh awareness of His unlimited supernatural power and the magnitude of His sacrifice when in His presence.

His eyes met mine; He knew my thoughts. Reaching into His pocket, He pulled out my white stone and held it out. "I believe this is yours, dear little sister."

The white stone seemed so unimportant next to Jesus. I couldn't speak.

He took my hand and walked with me to a nearby garden bench where He sweetly talked to me. "Camelia brought this to me. She said you take it wherever you go."

I nodded.

"I know you cherish this white stone because I gave it to you." He smiled and I basked euphorically in His flawless love. "Though material things in heaven do represent Our Father's glory, this white stone is not your treasure. The love behind the stone is your treasure. And Our love goes with you wherever you go."

He handed me the stone and kissed my forehead. Then He quietly rose and walked down the flower-lined path.

As He walked, I contemplated how true His words were.

Camelia chirped from a branch above my head.

"It was foolish of me to think you didn't know what you were doing, Camelia. Someday, you must show me what you do with all my ribbons."

She flapped her wings and flew around my head before disappearing in the sky.

Chapter 3 -- Chariots and Horsemen of Heaven

Walking down a path that closely followed a languidly flowing river, I stared wide-eyed at the passing scenery. The parks and homes were much lovelier than I had imagined while living on earth. Trees loaded with diverse fruits lined the river's banks. Alluring homes, some as big as castles, hid behind gardens, ornate trees and flowering shrubs.

As I walked, the landscape changed to an arid scene. Beautiful white-stone homes dotted the rocky terrain. The river grew very wide and flowering acacia trees now lined its banks. Glorious white lilies bordered the path before me. People sat by the river's edge engaged in conversation or singing. Others swam in the sparkling water.

Just then a wonderfully exciting thing happened. Horses, glowing like fire, came out of nowhere and pranced up to the river to drink. After drinking the sacred water, they rolled on the grassy bank.

I had always loved horses and wanted to pet them.

The lead horse gave the impression that he knew my thoughts when he stopped rolling and strutted toward me. As he drew close I backed away; light radiated from his body like swirling flames.

"It's all right," he assured me. "The fire-light won't hurt you. It's the power of God reflecting from me."

"You really talk!" I'd heard that some animals could talk in heaven. "It's amazing!" I reached out to pet him. "My mother has a donkey friend who talks, but I haven't met her yet."

The horse gave me a bemused look. "Surely you've read about Balaam's donkey?"

My face lit up remembering the story.

His lips curled up in a smile. "My name is Arman. Would you like a ride?"

"Oh yes! You can't imagine how much."

He bowed low and I climbed onto his back. When he stood up, he jolted into a run. I looked down and, sure enough, we were in the air. "Oh!" I cried, hanging tightly on to his neck. The other horses followed, racing across the sky. They flew so fast that I couldn't speak for a while.

At last, breathlessly, I said, "Please slow down. I'd like to see the land we're passing."

Arman's hoofs touched land before I finished speaking and he came to a halt. A stately mansion stood before us. A distinctive-looking horseman came out of a neighboring stable and led the other horses to their stalls. Afterward he took my hand and helped me down from Arman's back.

"I suppose you'd like to see the prophet." He turned and asked me to follow him. I silently followed, waving goodbye to Arman.

Who is the prophet? I wondered.

The horseman rang the mansion's doorbell and a tall gray-haired man came promptly to the door. His eyes were the brightest I had ever seen—except for Jesus'. Jesus' eyes sparkled more brilliantly than diamonds. "Elijah, you have a visitor," the horseman said.

My mouth fell open. I knew the man was the Elijah of the Old Testament.

Elijah smiled broadly and gave me a big hug. "Please come in."

He led me into a spacious sitting room of Middle Eastern decor. After I relaxed a little, I asked him about his life on earth. I especially wanted to know more about his stay at Kerith Brook, where the ravens fed him. Though he must have answered the question uncountable times, he answered as though it were the very first time. I marveled at his graciousness.

Afterward, he took me to a large gallery near the stables and showed me the chariots of heaven. "This is the one I rode in when I was parted from my young friend Elisha and brought home." He pointed to a beautiful chariot with gold wings extending from its sides.

We visited the stables next. Horsemen were feeding and brushing the horses. The horses all looked clean and well groomed, so I asked Elijah why they were being brushed.

He smiled and said, "For us, it's comforting and pleasurable to eat with one another." He looked at the gold ribbon in my hair and added, "Women enjoy putting flowers and ribbons in their hair to enhance their beauty. Then he motioned toward the horses and said, "They relish being fed and brushed. Of course, neither we nor the horses need to eat in heaven, but we enjoy eating. It's a special blessing. Would you like to feed them?"

I smiled with delight. As I fed them, they told me about their exciting trips to earth.

"We were there during many of the great wars," Arman whinnied.

"But no one ever saw you."

Elijah said, "I saw them. And my servant saw them. When God opens someone's eyes, he can see them."

I wanted to stay and ask them all about their earthly missions, but a word from the Father reminded me that I needed to continue my mission. I hugged my new friends and said goodbye.

Arman's radiant nose kissed my cheek. With his touch, I could feel the power of God pulsate through my body. "I'll take you for a ride up the Mount of Worship when God wills," he said.

"That will be wonderful!" I had never been on the heavenly Mount Zion. I hoped we would go soon.

Elijah showed me the path leading back to the river and I started out again for my appointment.

Waving goodbye as I walked, I thought, *He's such a warm, affectionate man—not at all like I imagined him while reading the Bible. Heaven has a way of changing everyone.* I wondered how much I had changed.

Chapter 4 -- The Mission

Crystal dishes sparkled and gold flatware gleamed on a glass table. Sweet cakes with cream on their sides filled a crystal platter while fresh fruit overflowed from a glistening gold bowl, giving the crowning touch. I had finally arrived at the home of one of the young girls to whom I was to minister.

Having prepared a brunch for me, she placed a clear glass near each of our plates. She was slim, with golden hair bouncing softly on her shoulders. She seemed energetic, almost to the point of restlessness. After asking me to sit, she seated herself across the table and looked at me.

Seeing discomfort in her eyes, I began our conversation. "What do you think of heaven, Lucian?"

Her eyes moistened. Looking at her surroundings, she said, "It's so beautiful! I keep asking myself why I'm so blessed."

I tried to comfort her. "Our Father loves us so much that it is indeed almost unbelievable." I put as much solace in my voice as I could.

It was obvious she had little understanding of God's love. She had come to this new land in very much the same spiritual condition she'd left earth. I asked her how she had come to believe in Jesus.

She hesitated at first, but recognized the love in my eyes and began to tell her story:

"I was raised by very devout Christian parents. We went to church every Sunday, morning and evening, and we had Bible studies and prayer meetings in our home every week. My parents were very strict." She gave me a thoughtful look. "Now, as I look back, I understand that they just wanted to spare me the troubles they had experienced. But at the time, I wanted my freedom. I wanted to enjoy life. I thought there had to be more to life than just God and church."

She stopped speaking and I followed her gaze to an ornately carved mahogany plant stand near the wall. An attractive arrangement of flowers decorated the pedestal. Baby's breath dominated the bouquet.

"Baby's breath was my mother's favorite." She mumbled. She wasn't sad. There is no sadness in heaven. She was just taken up in memories.

"I gave my parents a very difficult time with my rebellion," she went on. "But in spite of their sorrow, they kept getting closer to God. It was unnerving. The worse I became, the more they loved me. You can't imagine how annoying it was."

I smiled. I wanted to tell her all about how God's love works in us, but the Holy Spirit told me it was not yet time.

"Then one day," she continued, "I got very sick. For the first time, I realized I could die. I was terrified. My fear almost overcame me, until I started remembering verses I had learned in Sunday School. Things my parents had taught me flooded back. I asked Jesus to forgive my sins and promised to obey Him. The next thing I knew, I was here. Jesus warmly welcomed me, but I felt like I didn't really know Him."

I held her close. "Little sister, you have all eternity to get to know Jesus." I picked up my glass and told her to bring hers and follow me.

She looked at me questioningly but obediently picked up her glass and followed.

We walked through purple fields of plumgrass to a small hill. Upon cresting it, we beheld a tall fir tree with millions of gold ribbons. I stopped and stared at it. "Oh! Camelia, it's beautiful!"

Lucian looked at me quizzically again and asked, "Who's Camelia?"

"She's a dear bird companion of mine. What a marvelous job she's done decorating that tree. I must tell her when I see her." Her eyes opened wide. I didn't say any more but continued our walk, traveling through a small wood.

Coming upon a little cottage, I rang the doorbell and a young girl came to the door.

"You've finally come!" the girl exclaimed gleefully. Instead of inviting us in, she intuitively went back and grabbed a glass from her table and hurried to join us. "I'm so glad you've come! I know we'll all be great friends."

After closing the door behind her and giving us each a hug, she started skipping along a path. Lucian and I looked at each other and decided to skip along after her.

Reaching the base of a hill near her cottage, she stopped and turned back. "It was rude of me not to introduce myself. My name is Ruth." She extended her hand.

"I'm Lucian," replied my companion, taking her hand. The two, about the same age, smiled happily at each other. In their great joy of meeting each other they quickly forgot I was with them and started walking up the hill hand-in-hand. I followed.

When we reached the top, Ruth squealed, "There it is!" A glorious, winding river flowed through the valley below. We raced down to its bank. Its radiant water enraptured us; rays of light shone from its surface.

The girls eventually turned and looked at me expectantly. I dipped my glass into the river and filled it.

"Let's sit down for a while," I said.

The grass was very soft and Lucian feared it would stain her robe. Ruth assured her it wouldn't.

When they were settled, I began, "My dear sisters, these waters flow from the Throne Room of God." Their eyes opened wide. "It's living water; it is the very essence of God. Your Father wants you to drink it."

"What will happen to us?" Ruth asked apprehensively.

"The Father will commune with you." I poured some water in each of their glasses and we drank.

For a moment, there was silence. Then Ruth said to Lucian, "Have you started reading the Bible in your home?"

"I've started, but there's so much I don't understand."

"Let's read it together," Ruth suggested. "Jesus will help us understand it. I remember learning in Sunday School that He said He is the living water."

Before long, both talking at once, they left the river heading for Ruth's cottage.

When they were out of sight, I walked slowly into the river. Billows of Holy Spirit anointing began to flow through my body. I was glad the girls, too, would bathe in the Holy Spirit's presence. But for now, they would drink from the living Word.

Chapter 5 -- Power of Laughter

There was a part of heaven I had heard much about but had never seen. "May I go home through the Jubilee Jungle, Father?"

I heard the Father laugh and wondered what was so funny. Finally, He answered, "Yes, but I want you to go with Elaine."

"But Elaine's on earth."

"Your sister is on earth. The Elaine I'm speaking of lives near the Jubilee Jungle. I've told her you're coming."

Having a strong desire to get there as soon as possible, I no more than blinked and found myself there.

I wish I could be more patient! I probably missed some of the most glorious parts of heaven!

While berating myself, I noticed a dark-skinned woman approaching.

In a melodious, full voice, she said, "What a joy to meet you, dear sister." She squeezed me tightly.

"It's wonderful to meet you too," I chimed. "I have a sister named Elaine. She's still on earth."

"Yes, I know. I've heard she will arrive soon."

I clasped my hands. "I can't wait."

Elaine smiled and took my hand. "Come, let me show you the jungle."

We followed a trail into a dense growth of trees. Tall vegetation and vines canopied the path. "Are there wild animals in here?" I asked.

"None that would hurt you."

When we neared a clearing, we heard wild laughter coming from a large Kenya tree. On its branches we spied very unusual animals. I drew closer for a better look and stared up at them. They had the body and head of a monkey, but the tail and ears of a rabbit. They became perfectly still.

"What are they?" I asked.

"Why don't ya ask us?" one of the creatures squawked.

"Oh, please forgive me. I didn't know you could speak."

They laughed and rolled on the branches.

"They're called bunkeys," Elaine said, "for reasons you can see. I think you need to get to know these little fellows. I'll leave you alone with them for a while." She retreated into the jungle in the same direction from which we'd come.

I wasn't at all sure I wanted to get to know these little creatures; they were so strange. I looked back up the tree. Dozens of little eyes looked back at me.

"Well, what ya wait'n for? C'mon up," one of them challenged. I must have had a shocked expression because every bunkey contorted its face in feigned shock. I smiled at their impersonations. They smiled back.

This is crazy, I thought, and shook my head. The bunkeys shook their heads. They shook them so fiercely that the whole tree jiggled.

"Oh, please," I said with a laugh. "Stop, I'll come up."

Halfway up the tree, while grasping a small limb, my hand slipped and I fell to the ground. I wasn't hurt, just surprised.

All the bunkeys then jumped to the ground and started climbing one by one back up the tree. Halfway up, each fell to the ground and lay there with a surprised look on its face. I laughed. As their parade continued, I kept laughing. I couldn't stop. The bunkeys laughed and laughed too.

Fortunately, Elaine came back and helped me back onto my feet. As we walked back into the Jungle, my laughter turned to praise: "Oh Father, thank You for those wonderful creatures."

I had laughed so hard that my legs felt weak. Tears rolled down my cheeks; yet, I felt new strength. "Thank You, Father, for the joy of laughter."

I said to Elaine, "Now I know why the Father laughed when I asked to come here."

She smiled knowingly and sang, "The joy of the Lord is my strength."

We could still hear the bunkeys laughing when we reached the clearing. Elaine told me they would keep falling out of the tree, acting surprised and laughing for quite a while.

"Hopefully not eternity," I chuckled.

"No, they'll have some new performance for their next visitor. The Father has a mission for every creature in heaven. That's their mission."

Before long we were out of the jungle and back at the spot where we'd met, having been in deep conversation about the goodness of God along the way.

"Speaking of the Father," I said, "I sense I need to be on my way. I'm excited about preparing for my sister's arrival." We hugged goodbye.

I was laughing again while walking home, when suddenly I realized someone was walking beside me. I looked up to see it was Jesus. His eyes were full of merriment.

"I thought you might like for your sister to be welcomed

by the bunkeys when she arrives." I laughed and He laughed with me.

We visited for a moment and then He put His hand on my head and said "Walk in My power and My anointing" before walking away.

Walking on by myself, I thought, *I didn't react as I usually do when I meet Jesus. Have I grown spiritually?*

Chapter 6 -- A Great Race

Resting in my heavenly home where I reposed between mission trips was wonderful. Jesus had told the workmen exactly how to build it. Each room, each piece of furniture, each item pleased me immensely. I couldn't thank God enough. I lay on my window seat praising Him until my eyes closed with the sensation of being engulfed in His love.

Loud chirping woke me from my sweet sleep. Camelia, perched on the window box, did her best to get my attention.

"Camelia, I believe you have a problem with letting me sleep."

While chirping at me, she tilted her head to the right and left. I was sure she was trying to figure out why she could understand me but I couldn't understand her. She flew to my arm and tugged on my sleeve with her beak.

"I gather you want to show me something."

She nodded.

"Well then," I smiled, "let's go."

As soon as I said go, she was gone.

"Camelia," I cried after her, "I can't follow you if you fly that fast."

In two seconds she was back.

Camelia flew as slowly as she could while I ran after her. We ran out of the house and down the golden path. Every few seconds she turned to see if I was coming. She even flew back to pull on my robe and hurry me along occasionally.

Of all the people in heaven, I believed I was the most impatient. And I felt Camelia must have been unequaled among all the creatures of creation in the same shortcoming. *I suppose that's why we're such good friends*, I thought. *God must have sent you to teach me patience. I have no doubt I'm your lesson in patience.*

We traversed a field of wild flowers, crossed a brook and climbed a hill before stopping on the edge of a grassy plain.

Fire-like horses similar to the ones I had met by the river stood in array before us. With them were the cherubim Ezekiel described in the Old Testament as the four living creatures who stand before the Throne of God. I had heard a great deal about them, but I had never seen them. I stood in awe of them. Each cherub had four wings and four faces: the face of a man, a lion, an ox and an eagle. Their bodies were like lit torches. Fire swirled all around them.

Arman instructed them along with the other horses:

"I'm confident this next exercise will prove very enjoyable. We're going to race around that mountain"—he pointed his nose at a distant mountain—"and come back to this finish line." He drew a long line in the soft ground with his front hoof. The horses of fire and living creatures agreed that it would be fun.

Lightning flashed out from them as they lined up on the starting line. God's power was so strong around them that it never occurred to me to try to move closer.

I noticed that the living creatures each had a wheel within a wheel on the ground beside them. The rims of the wheels were full of eyes. Amazed at what I saw, I vaguely heard a voice say, "On your mark."

Camelia, on the loftiest limb of a tall tree nearby, began to chirp excitedly.

"Get set. Go." Clapping wings were as deafening as the roar of a tornado. The horses and living creatures vanished like flashes of lightning.

A few moments later they appeared as glowing streaks coming back from the mountain toward the finish line. But a fraction of a second before crossing the finish line, they came to complete halts and stood there as though they'd turned into statues.

Strutting up and down the finish line was Camelia, her wings raised in victory. She had joined the race at the last millisecond and now danced around as if she had won some great trophy or grand prize. The cherubim and horses of fire stared at her in bewilderment.

Jesus appeared and lovingly picked Camelia up and held her in his hand while smiling at the other contenders.

Camelia flew up and kissed His cheek thankfully. She had won the race with His help.

With God, all things are possible, I thought.

Everyone smiled. It was a great lesson they had learned.

But then I thought, *Oh no, I'll never hear the end of this.*

Jesus looked at me knowingly, but patiently.

I remembered I couldn't understand Camila and smiled sheepishly. I also was learning a lesson.

Chapter 7 -- The Homecoming

The house was almost completed. White columns enclosed the front porch. Fruit trees of various kinds mingled with flowering bushes and circular gardens in the courtyard. Inside, the rooms exuded light and warmth.

I looked out huge arched windows dominating the east wall of her studio. They framed a majestic, clear view of the Mount of Worship. *She will love this room*, I assured myself. While studying the golden light illuminating the mount, a prayer of praise welled up in my spirit.

Some small children playing outside noticed me staring at the mount. "The golden rays will soon turn to all colors of the rainbow," a boy said. "Whenever Jesus enters the Throne Room, God's glory radiates from the mount."

Camelia flew in through the window to perch on my shoulder. Facing the Mount of Worship, she remained very quiet—very unlike Camelia. I realized she was praying.

"Can we help you get the house ready for your sister?" a little girl asked.

"Oh, I would like that very much."

They ran off.

"I wonder where they're going," I said to Camelia. Camelia didn't hear me. She had flown out the window after the children. *She is such a precious bird.*

When I turned, I saw Elaine standing in the doorway across the room. I could tell she had been with Jesus; glory shone from her face. I walked over and took her hands gently in mine. Tears of joy cascaded down her cheeks as I looked into her eyes. I hugged her.

Looking up she discovered the Mount of Worship. The sky flooded with every color imaginable while angels sang rhapsodies of praises. Elaine lifted her hands and turned round and round in praise with the melody.

Camelia and the children returned carrying wreaths of flowers. They placed them on their heads before dancing around the room in praise with Elaine. Camelia gently placed a wreath on Elaine's head. The studio became a ballroom of worship.

Too soon, the sky changed back to a golden light and the angels' singing sounded farther in the distance. Elaine stared at the Mount of Worship. After a while, she turned to speak to the children, wanting to thank them, but she couldn't find any words.

They understood. Taking the wreaths off their heads, they placed them around the room adorning furniture before silently leaving the house.

Camelia wasn't ready to quit dancing. She flew to the middle of the room and raised her wings in praise. When she wiggled her little body, Elaine and I laughed.

Elaine tenderly picked her up and carried her to the window. They stared together at the Mount of Worship.

Camelia had found a new friend.

Not one word had been spoken between my sister and me, yet each of us had understood the other's heart. Silently, I too left the house; she needed to be alone with God. We would have all eternity to talk.

My sister, my friend, had come home.

Chapter 8 -- The Garden

A lovely stone mill home nestled under evergreen branches deep in a forest. Water meandered over its mill wheel and poured back into a small creek. I needed to cross a footbridge to reach the door.

I had visited often since my arrival in heaven. My mother enjoyed preparing dinner for me and walking with me among her flowers. This time Elaine had joined us. After our meal, Mother was determined to show her every garden.

She said, "Elaine, dear, I've planted a garden especially for you. Its flowers have doubled in size and beauty since the last time your sister was here." She walked out the back door and Elaine and I followed her to a clearing in the forest where we feasted our senses on gardens of every flower conceivable.

"Gardens in heaven don't need weeding," mother said. "The soil occasionally needs to be loosened around the flowers' roots for air and water. Have you noticed the marvelous air here?"

We couldn't tell which of us she was asking; so we both breathed in deeply and smiled. The air imparted the sweet presence of God.

"Yes," mother continued, reading our expressions, "how can anything not grow beautifully in this air?" She touched the flowers gently as she walked ahead of Elaine and me. "The water in the creek comes straight from the Sacred River. As often as the Father tells me, I bring water from the creek and water the flowers."

"That must be an awful lot of work," I noted, mentally measuring the gardens.

"Oh, Martha helps me," she assured me. She then started telling Elaine about her donkey friend, Martha.

"Have you come for flowers for the Throne Room?" A deep voice asked. We turned to behold a small gray donkey.

"This," Mother said, "is Martha."

"I'm sorry," I said. "We didn't come for flowers for the Throne Room; we came to see Mother's lovely gardens."

Martha lowered her head and walked over to a nearby tree where she lay down. "Jesus stood right here not long ago," she moped. "He came for flowers for the Throne Room." Her eyes filled with tears.

Mother explained: "Martha wasn't here when He came. Another donkey received the honor of carrying flowers up the Mount of Worship for Jesus."

Elaine walked over to stroke Martha's neck. "He'll be back again soon," she said, running her hand gently over her hide. Martha was not easily consoled.

"I'll show you where he picked flowers," Mother bragged. We followed her to a garden where we beheld the most beautiful flowers we had ever seen. They had the appearance of jasper and carnelian.

"The colors that radiate from God," I whispered. Their delicate fragrance of praise perfumed the air. I inhaled as much as I could.

Out of the corner of my eye I noticed Martha getting up. When she began to stagger down the edge of a garden, Mother observed her also. Mother's eyes widened with fear and her legs began to wobble. I braced her.

Martha let out a loud bray and then fell to the ground. She rolled over and lay motionless with her four feet straight up in the air. Mother darted over to her. Elaine and I followed.

"Did she die?" Mother cried.

"You shouldn't bother a dying donkey," Martha told her sternly. She rolled over and got back onto her feet, then shook soil off her mane. She brayed, "It hurts dying to self! Now, I have to go and thank that donkey for helping Jesus." With a lifted spirit, she pranced out of the garden.

"I don't know if I'll ever understand that donkey," Mother said, having regained her composure. "Of course, I knew she didn't die: nothing dies in heaven. But she pulls the strangest tricks on me."

It was time for Elaine and me to leave. We kissed and hugged Mother goodbye.

I sang a song of praise for Martha as I walked home.

The Father spoke to my heart: *There will be a day when your mother understands Martha.*

I smiled. *I know.*

Chapter 9 -- Visitors

The doorbell rang a lovely melody and I rose to see who had come. As I opened the door, the girls yelled, "Surprise!"

I was surprised to see Ruth and Lucian smiling brightly.

"Oh, please come in," I sang as I hugged each of them. I motioned them into the parlor. They giggled.

"We were down by the Sacred River praising God," Ruth began, "when all of a sudden we both had a strong desire to see you. We asked God about it and, while the words were still on our lips, a breeze came and picked us up. We floated all the way here!" They laughed with delight.

"You can't imagine what we saw on the way!" Lucian thrilled. "We passed over a bright red place!"

"We've no idea what it was," Ruth added.

"It's a Valentine Garden," I informed them. "You really must see it someday." At that, they were in rapture.

When they calmed down, Lucian went on, "We passed over the Golden Sea. Did you know there's a whale in the sea?"

"No, I didn't know that."

Camelia flew into the parlor and lighted on a table. "What a beautiful bird!" Ruth gasped.

Lucian agreed. "You are so pretty, little bird." She tried to pet her.

Camelia would have none of it; she flew to another spot and bent her head from side to side looking at them while they cooed over her. Then she flew back out the window.

"Why did she leave so quickly?" Ruth asked.

"She's having a little trouble with humility since winning the great race." Of course, Ruth didn't have any idea what I was talking about.

Her eyes popped open round as hickory nuts and she gushed, "Oh! We almost forgot to tell you. The Father said we could see the live movie of the life of Moses! I saw the movie, *The Ten Commandments,* once. Moses was awesome in it!" Lucian again agreed. Ruth went on, "We'll even get to meet Moses! In fact, he's going to show the movie!"

"The live movie of Moses' life is indeed wonderful," I said, "much better than the movie you saw on earth. But Moses has a difficult time showing it; he finds it very humbling."

"That can't be right," Lucian contended. "Moses was the most humble man on earth—the Bible says so."

"Yes," I said, "but when he watches the movie of his life, he sees how short he falls in humility compared to Jesus."

The girls, again not understanding, just looked at me.

"I guess that's why the Father asked him to show the movie," I said, more to myself than to them.

With sympathy and determination, Ruth said, "We'll encourage him; tell him how wonderful we think he is."

"Yes, we'll praise him profusely," Lucian chimed.

Knowing their praise would only increase Moses' embarrassment, I wondered if I should discourage them. The Holy Spirit showed me how the end result would be even greater humility, so I said, "That would be lovely, girls."

Camelia flew into the room again. Seeing that the girls were still there, she did a quick loop and flew straight back out.

"Come back here pretty bird," Ruth shouted after her. Camelia was already far away.

"I've never seen a bird fly so fast!" Lucian declared.

I sensed the girls needed to be on their way, so I thanked them for coming and walked them to my courtyard gate.

After hugging them goodbye, I walked back to my colonnaded porch and up its marble steps. I glanced back before opening my front door and was surprised to see them still standing just outside the gate. I surmised that they were wondering how to get home.

I hollered, "Ask the Father; He'll get you home."

They bowed their heads and a breeze came and carried them away. I could hear them laughing as they floated over the trees.

"Goodbye," they yelled back. "Come and see us."

Camelia, having returned to a courtyard tree, shook her head no

Chapter 10 -- Crown With a Nest

It was an especially glorious time in heaven. The air tingled with the Holy Spirit's power. People and animals busily prepared for the time of worship during the great celebration. Mother had many helping with her floral arrangements. Shopkeepers in the business district produced banners and flags. Soon, every resident of heaven would climb the Mount of Worship for a wonderful time of joy, laughter and praise.

I, too, needed to get things in order for the celebration. My festive robe shimmered hanging neatly on its golden hook. I took it down and smoothed it gently with my hand. It sparkled even brighter with my touch.

I wouldn't have needed an iron if I had had this power on earth. Oh, the hours I spent ironing! They had actually been good times: times of worship, songs and prayer. I had even been filled with the Holy Spirit while ironing.

Snapping back to the present, I told myself to keep my mind on what I was doing. My robe in order, I remembered my crown.

It had been a very humbling experience the first time Jesus placed it on my head. *There's no way I deserve such a beautiful crown,"* I'd thought, and handed it back to Him. With great love, He'd told me, "This crown is a symbol of My Father's work accomplished in you. By wearing it, you glorify Him." With smiling eyes, He added, "And it would please me very much." With reciprocal love, I'd taken it back and placed it on my head. "That's better," He'd beamed.

At the great celebration, we would all place our crowns at Jesus' feet—because it was He who had made it possible for us to come to heaven. He would give them back to us as His way of glorifying the Father. We never tired of the ceremony; it was drenched in the Holy Spirit's love and anointing.

When I took my crown from the shelf, I noticed grass attached to its base. Looking closely, I was astonished to find a dainty little nest. A gold ribbon had been used to intertwine the grass with the crown.

"Camelia!" I said loudly. "You have made a beautiful nest! But in my crown!"

Camelia didn't show herself. I had noticed her looking at my crown several times, but I never dreamed she'd make a nest in it.

"Oh, dear Father, what will I do?" My prayer was more of exasperation than of petition. "I must wear my crown for the celebration!"

"Wear the crown with the nest in it," the Father directed.

My jaw dropped. Surely I hadn't heard Him right. *How can I wear my crown to such a glorious event with a nest in it? What would all of heaven think of me?*

Knowing my true need, the Father added, "Let Camelia sit in it."

Tears filled my eyes as I pictured how ridiculous I would look,

A gentle breeze of the Spirit came through the window bringing peace to my heart. I began to see how foolish I was to concern myself with what others might think of me while doing what the Father asked.

"Will I ever get rid of these earthly thoughts?" I asked.

"Yes, my daughter."

Chapter 11 -- Ride to the Mount of Worship

"We'll be leaving for the Mount of Worship soon," I told Elaine. She was walking around in a stupor from thinking about the celebration.

She said, "My legs feel weak from anticipation. I wonder if I'll even be able to climb the mount."

The air was so full of God's power that everyone felt weak under it. Experiencing God's anointing had always been that way for me on earth, but I had expected it to feel different in my new body. I reminded myself that God's power was much stronger here, especially during celebrations. *My body of flesh wouldn't even have been able to function here.*

The neighing of horses joltingly interrupted my thoughts. Elaine darted to the window. When she backed away, I looked out and saw Arman and some of his friends pawing the air. I understood why she'd backed away: they were aglow with fire brighter than usual. They had come prepared for the celebration with wreaths of flowers around their necks.

When I opened the door, Arman asked, "Are you ready?" Seeing I didn't understand, he explained: "I told you I'd take you for a ride up the Mount of Worship."

Excitement rushed through my being. "Elaine," I sputtered. "We have a ride up the mount!"

She stared speechlessly at the horses.

"Hurry, they're waiting." My prodding was enough to break her trance. We rushed around the room gathering our crowns and palm branches. Picking up my crown, I remembered Camelia. "Where's Camelia?"

Elaine pointed to a tree outside.

"Camelia, dear," I called, "we have to go."

Quick as lightning she shot through the window and sat in her nest. Elaine and I laughed.

We placed our crowns on our heads and went outside. I mounted Arman and Elaine mounted one of his friends.

"We're going to stop by our stable and follow Elijah's chariots up the mount," Arman informed us.

It was almost more excitement than I could bear. We would see everything—a great improvement over my previous ride when all of the scenery flew by in a blur. "Hang on," I shouted to Elaine as the horses leapt into the air.

Camelia sat in her nest, enjoying the ride, I think. I felt her little body tremble now and then. I knew she would rather be flying. She could beat these horses up the mount. *That might be why the Father asked her to ride,* I thought. *And Camelia humbly obeyed!*

Millions of angels and flying creatures flew to the summit over the heads of millions of people walking. Music filled the air and angelic choirs joined the saints in song.

We spotted Mother riding Martha. Her closest friend rode a donkey beside her. They carried baskets overflowing with flowers. We waved and they nodded back. Mother blew us a kiss.

At the summit, people danced in praise beneath a row of golden palm trees. Elaine was elated to see the dancers. Beyond them, pure white light, brighter than the sun, surrounded the Throne Room, rendering it nearly invisible. An enormous, solid-gold vestibule protruded from the light in our direction. We referred to it fondly as Ezekiel's vestibule.

Our rides secured us inside and then left. We waited just inside the entrance for Mother and her friend.

Shortly after they arrived hundreds of trumpets rent the air. Everyone trembled. It was time to enter the Throne Room. As soon as the heavenly masses were assembled within, we fell prostrate before Jesus as He ascended His throne. A spirit of total surrender permeated each being. Everyone placed his or her crown at Jesus' feet. Blessed events followed which could not have been understood by people still on earth.

After the ceremony Jesus gave each person's crown back. A loving smile traveled over His face as He placed mine on my head. He touched Camelia's head and blessed her. Elaine and I lingered a while in the sweet spirit of adoration. When we went outside, we were pleasantly surprised to find Arman waiting for us. Elaine breathed a sigh of relief. She said, "I feel so exhausted from the anointing that I'm glad we have a ride down the mount."

Changing the subject, she asked, "Did you notice how wonderfully Camelia sang throughout the celebration?" I shook my head. I had been so taken up with Jesus that I hadn't noticed anything or anyone else.

We found Mother and kissed her goodbye before mounting our rides. I noticed Camelia was lying very still in her nest, so I took my crown off and peeked in. There she was—sound asleep. *She's so precious.*

"I guess she wore herself out," I said to Elaine.

She smiled and said, "I'm looking forward to a nap too."

Off we went into the sky.

Chapter 12 -- The Rock

I rested in my home with much to think about after my trip to the mount, and much to talk to the Father about. I lifted a prayer for my children and husband as I often did. Just as I had hung on to God's promises for them while on earth, I kept those same promises in my heart here in heaven. "They will all serve You, Father," I confirmed.

Glancing out a window, I detected an unusual glow in the sky. No birds singing. No children playing. No activity of any kind. *Everyone must still be overwhelmed from the celebration,* I thought. Camelia was still sleeping in my crown. *What an experience for her.*

It occurred to me that this would be the perfect time to go to the Golden Sea. I could rest on the beach and watch the waves caress the shore.

With a prayer to the Father, I was standing on the sandy edge of a bay. I scanned the massive body of water. It filled my heart with the awesomeness of God.

On earth, the ocean had frightened me. But here there was nothing to fear. The sea never took on the dark colors of the sky; it stayed vibrantly crystal clear. And the sky was dependably golden tone, its reflection gloriously soft gold.

Gazing at the farthest reaches of the sea, I noticed movement. *What is that?* Squinting, I made out the whale the girls had told me about. My heart filled with praise.

"Praise be to God the Father, dear whale," I cried.

To my surprise, the whale swam toward me. When he reached shore, he invited me in a playful, bubbly voice to climb onto his back. "The Father told me to take you somewhere," he reassured me.

I listened for the Father.

"Go."

Curious and excited, I waded out and climbed onto the whale's back. I sensed the creature's great power. As soon as I found a good grip on his slippery skin, he swam so far out to sea that we couldn't see land anymore.

I spotted a large rock jutting up from the sea. The whale swam over to it and said, "Here you are."

I was perplexed, but I slid off the whale onto the rock. I climbed to its top and looked out over the sea.

The whale swam off into the distance.

Watching the waves rise and fall, I began to feel alone and sad. I thought of my son, David. "I am a rock," he'd often said. Looking down, I noted that the rock was barren of life.

The Golden Sea had always been very calm, but now a wind began to blow and waves started braking against the rock. I hung on and braced myself against the wind. As it grew stronger and waves crashed over the rock, God's power kept me from washing away.

At last the wind subsided. I was soaking wet. I looked down at the rock again and discovered moss in its crevices. The sea had brought new life from the Holy Spirit.

The whale surfaced close to the rock and, thankfully, I crawled onto his back. He headed back toward shore.

Jesus was waiting on the shore. The whale brought me close enough so I could slide off and walk over to Him. He took my hands in His and said, "Underneath the rock on which you stood was a much larger rock which held it in place. As the winds and waves of the Holy Spirit beat against the top rock, its smooth outer crust cracked and life was able to take hold and grow in its crevices." Squeezing my hand, he said, "I hold that rock in place." He looked deep into my eyes and added, "David knows that I am *the* Rock."

We sat on the shore. While Jesus looked out at the sea, my eyes stayed on Him. He turned and said once more, "David knows I am the unchanging and immutable Rock."

My heart was so filled with gratefulness that I wept. I stammered, "Thank You for loving him so."

He rose and told me He'd walk me home.

I stood and waved goodbye to the whale. The whale spouted water into the air and the spray landed right on me, flooding me with joy.

Jesus and I laughed then headed for my home.

Chapter 13 -- Daniel and the Lions

Sitting quietly at my desk with my Bible lying open, I gazed reflectively out the window. Meditating on My Father's Word had filled my heart with joy. But then I thought, *How many people on earth don't believe this book is true?"* Tears filled my eyes.

The Father lifted my sorrow when I heard children laugh in the distance. Their laughter reminded me of the Jubilee Jungle. *Who might the bunkeys be imitating now*, I wondered.

Looking again at my Bible, I thought about other animals it mentioned. "Are there lions in heaven, Father? No one has mentioned them." *Come to think of it, I didn't see them on the Mount of Worship—and all of heaven was there. Yet, Jesus was called the Lion of Judah.*

Realizing that the Father hadn't answered, I looked up at the Mount of Worship. The sky above the mount revolved in a magnificent display of colors. I knew Jesus was speaking with the Father and my answer would come later.

Shortly, the Father answered: "Yes, there are lions in heaven, and soon you may visit them."

I giggled like a child at a circus.

The sound of children's laughter again captured my attention. I decided to walk to the park where they played. Sitting on the grass near the river, I watched them chase one another. A small boy stopped now and then to study me. Finally, he cautiously approached me. I could tell he hadn't been in heaven long.

"Hello there." I said, trying to put him at ease.

He timidly asked, "Are you the lady who's going to take me to see the lions?"

I smiled as the Father showed me Jesus telling him I would take him to see some Lions. "Yes," I told the boy. "We will have a wonderful time."

Jumping up and down, he begged excitedly, "Can we go

now?"

I laughed. "Yes." I took his hand and led him along the river's edge toward the jungle.

My small charge talked about wild animals he had seen during his short time on earth. "A cougar killed our dog Rex," he mourned.

"None of the animals here will hurt you," I assured him.

He wasn't convinced. As we neared the jungle, he started tugging on my sleeve. "Have you seen these lions?"

"No," I admitted. "But the Father says even a lamb can lie down by them and not be hurt."

"What about a boy?"

"If they won't hurt a lamb, they won't hurt a boy either."

"Have ya come tah visit us?" a voice spoke from the jungle.

We looked up and to our surprise the trees were full of bunkeys. They started laughing and rolling on the branches. My little traveling companion laughed with them.

"We've come to see the lions," I told them.

A few bunkeys jumped down from the trees. "We'll take ya to 'em," one said. With that, they ran off into the jungle, checking back occasionally to monitor our progress.

I held the boy's hand tightly as we ran along a path after them. We passed a lengthy stretch of thick vegetation before coming upon a small meadow where three lions enjoyed a rest sprawled out on the grass.

The bunkeys charged at them fearlessly. They climbed onto their backs and pulled their manes and tails. The lions stood up, but the bunkeys clung to their backs. The perturbed lions walked around the grassy prairie with the bunkeys laughing hysterically on their backs.

Pulling on the boy's hand, I urged him to meet the lions. He planted his feet and refused to move. Searching for a better tactic, I asked, "What's your name?"

"Daniel."

"Daniel!" I repeated.

He nodded.

I hid my amusement. With a steady voice I told him, "Daniel, the lions won't hurt you. See how they're playing with the bunkeys."

About this time the lions had had enough. Roaring ferociously they shook the bunkeys off their backs. The little animals headed for the trees. Daniel hid behind me.

"Father, what am I to do?"

I heard the bleating of a sheep; a small lamb approached the lions. A large, male lion welcomed it by licking its face. Lying down together, the lamb cuddled up next to the lion.

"Thank You, Father."

Daniel still refused to meet the lions. I looked back at the lion and lamb hoping to find some inspiration. With great relief I saw Jesus standing beside them.

Daniel saw Him too. With a squeal of delight he ran to Him.

Jesus picked him up and twirled him around in the air. They both laughed so hard that they fell to the ground. A lion came over and licked Daniel's face. Daniel chuckled and hugged him in return.

"Perfect love casts out all fear," I said to the Father.

"Yes."

After a short talk with Daniel, Jesus picked him up and placed him on a lion's back. He picked up the lamb and placed it over His own shoulders. Then He thanked me and said, "We're going to take the lamb back to the flock." He and the lion turned and walked away.

I hollered after Daniel, "Come visit me."

Daniel smiled back at me before disappearing behind some bushes.

Chapter 14 -- Gina

I could barely keep up with her. Her vigor for climbing the hill belied her age. Though having been much older than I, Gina had been my close friend since our earth days. In spite of the easier descent, I continued to labor to breathe until we finally reached the shore of Noah's Lake.

"Has anyone ever told you you must be related to Moses?" I teased. "He stayed strong right up to a hundred and twenty."

She laughed. "You know there's no physical age in heaven. Besides, it's our spiritual age that matters." She was right of course. In heaven, age is measured by spiritual growth.

While thinking about what she'd said, I noticed her eyeing something out on the lake. Tears formed in her eyes.

"Oh! Father," she said. "It's so beautiful! Thank You." I scanned the lake. All I could see was water.

"Oh! Father, it's so beautiful! Thank You," she said again, and again. She sat down on the sand and buried her face in her hands.

"Are you okay?"

"I'm so full of joy I'm afraid I might burst." She took a moment to collect herself. "What the Father showed me was so beautiful!"

"Well, tell me what it was before *I* burst with curiosity."

"Remember when I saw Jesus walking on the water when we were on earth?"

I nodded.

"Well, I just had that same vision. Jesus was—" She stopped in mid-sentence and stared out at the lake. I followed her gaze to see Jesus walking on the water toward us. He was not alone. A man and woman conversed with Him as they walked. Before long, we could hear their conversation.

"I always wanted to walk on water," the man said. The

woman laughed, hanging tightly on to Jesus' arm.

We stood when they reached shore.

Jesus hugged Gina and me. "Peace to you, Sisters." He introduced the couple to me and then to Gina.

"This is Gina. She'll help you feel at home here."

Gina's face radiated with love. She gave each of them a big hug. "First," she said, "I must show you your new homes."

They looked at Jesus.

He nodded.

Jesus and I watched them walk toward the hill. They seemed to relax as they chatted.

After a few moments, Jesus sat down on a large rock and looked out over the water. I sat on the sand near His feet.

"They don't know anyone in heaven," He said. "The Father brought them home shortly after they believed. Gina is the perfect one to make them feel welcomed."

I smiled. "You prepared her on earth for her ministry. She couldn't love people enough."

"Yes," He said. "And I also prepared you. After Gina gets them situated and more at ease, I'd like you to help them understand My Word."

"I will."

He smiled. "Have I told you how glad We are that you are here?"

My eyes moistened. "A thousand times," I said, laughing.

Jesus laughed too. He placed His hand on my head and said, "Go in My anointing." Then He disappeared.

Not knowing where Gina had taken Heidi and John, I asked the Father. Immediately, I found myself standing at the door of a house. I rang the doorbell. Heidi opened the door and joyfully held out her hand. "Please come in."

"You have a beautiful home."

She blushed. While Gina conversed with John, I asked her, "How did you come to believe in Jesus?"

She smiled and invited me to sit down, then told her story:

The other night while John and I had some drinks and shared some marijuana, I noticed the street in front of our apartment filling up with cars. People were flocking to the church on the corner across the street. I mentioned it to John.

He looked out the window. "Another revival meeting! "What do they do over there?" he asked laughingly. I expected him to say something derogatory about them, but he said, "Let's go find out."

What a lark, I thought. We staggered out the door and crossed the street.

Attempting to be as inconspicuous as possible, we found a couple of vacant seats in the back pew. The preacher vigorously paced the floor as he spoke. He seemed so nervous that I laughed to myself. John laughed quietly under his breath too.

Suddenly the preacher stopped and looked straight at John and me. He pointed his finger right at us and said, "Jesus brought you here to save your souls." Everyone looked at us. I wanted to get up and run, but I was glued to the seat.

He then began to tell us how Jesus had died for our sins. "You need to step out in faith and believe in the Lord Jesus Christ!" he thundered. "Don't be afraid. Walk on the water with Jesus."

Without any warning, Jesus appeared at the end of our pew with His hands reaching out to us. We both saw Him. There was so much love in His eyes that I immediately rose and took His hand. John took His other hand. The floor beneath us turned to water and we walked on it to the front of the church. There at the altar, we gave our hearts to Jesus.

At this point, Heidi became too emotional to speak. I waited, feeling her emotion. After a moment, she went on:

Back at home, we both thought we had hallucinated. But the next morning I felt different. There was a new peace in my heart that I had never felt before. John said he felt it in his heart too. Both of us could remember every word the preacher had said.

"It wasn't from the booze and weed," John determined. "It really happened!" We hugged and cried for joy. We each felt like a completely different person.

The next day, we had plans to fly to John's parents' home. I said to him, "I wonder if they'll notice we're different."

On the plane, I remember the pilot announcing that we were experiencing some difficulties. A little later, he told us to prepare for an emergency landing."

With her face mirroring her disbelief, Heidi whispered:

"I felt so at peace. Then we were here."

Her story ended.

I repeated the words to her that Jesus had spoken to me: "Have I told you how glad we are that you're here?"

We cried and hugged.

When Gina and John joined us, Gina lovingly told Heidi, "You need time to rest now. Lie down. We'll come by later with a lunch. I've made some delicious biscuits and some fruit jam."

Gina bubbled with exuberance. Ministering to others

always exhilarated her. We all hugged before she and John started out for John's new home.

I told her, "I think I'll go home and rest too."

"Yes, you do that, dear one." She smiled. "I love you."

"I love you too."

"We're all meeting back here for lunch," she reminded me.

As I walked home, I pictured again Heidi and John walking with Jesus on the water. I knew Gina had always loved the water because it reminded her of both the Father and Jesus. *What wonderful memories she will have.*

Chapter 15 — A Talking Flower

I knelt by my chair with hands lifted, lost in a world of praise. The doorbell curtailed my rapt state. The Father would usually tell me when someone was coming to visit. This time He hadn't. I opened the door to find Elaine. She had such a huge smile that I almost had to laugh.

"Come in, come in."

"I have to tell you what happened at Mother's gardens. It's so exciting!"

I invited her into the parlor and motioned for her to sit. Pulling up a chair beside her, I leaned forward eagerly. This is what she told me:

> While I was helping Mother with her flowers, the Father sent me on a mission. It turned out

to be a rather lengthy one. When I got back, I stopped at Mother's.

Instead of taking me right to the gardens like she usually does, she asked me to sit with her in her kitchen. I could tell she was troubled and asked what was wrong.

She looked at me hesitantly, then said, "I know this may sound uncharitable, but there's a flower in my Joy Garden that's really getting on my nerves."

I said, "In your Joy Garden?" Isn't that the one with mostly roses?" She nodded. "What could the flower possibly be doing?"

Obviously frustrated, she said, "It will not stop talking."

"It talks?"

"Yes, it talks. Have you ever seen or heard of a talking flower since you've been in heaven?"

"Yes, I've heard of them, but I've never seen one."

She got up and began to pace the floor. "It never stops talking, Elaine."

"What does it say?"

"That's what's so maddening. It's some foreign earthly or heavenly language; I can't understand a word of it."

"I can see how that could get on your nerves. What does Martha think of it?"

"Oh you know Martha. She just says 'Amen, Amen and Amen' every time she passes it. I don't know which one bothers me more." She threw her hands up.

When I motioned for her to have a seat again, she complied and said, "I know I shouldn't be this way."

I asked if she'd spoken to Jesus or the Father about the flower. She shook her head and said,

"They have so much to do in heaven and on earth; I don't want to bother them with such a silly thing. It is silly, isn't it?" She went on without waiting for my answer. "I know I should be overjoyed, and I was at first. I invited all my friends over to see it. They were all blessed, but no one understood what it was saying. Finally, its constant talking got to be too much."

"May I see the flower?" I asked. "If Martha is agreeing with it, she must know what it's saying,"

"I asked Martha if she understood it and she said no. But if you want to see it, I'll show it to you."

As we neared the Joy Garden, we heard Martha saying, "Amen, Amen and Amen." The flower was so beautiful! It was an exquisite, dainty rose. When I listened carefully to its tiny, sweet voice, I couldn't believe my ears. My eyes filled with tears. I told Mother, "It's speaking Hebrew."

Mother stared openmouthed at the rose. "What is it saying?"

I listened a moment and then told her. "It's saying, 'I praise You Father for this beautiful sister who gives me living water. I praise You Father for her loving touch as she passes me. Praise You that she loosens the soil around my roots. Bless her with abundant love.'" I couldn't help but cry.

Mother cried too. Then she said, "You'd think the Father would tell me it was praying."

I hugged her and told her, "You need to go to the Father with everything, Mother. Nothing is too small. That's how you build a relationship with Him." She smiled through her tears, understanding.

Her story told, Elaine said, "I had to come over to tell you. Isn't it beautiful!?"

Chapter 16 -- Burning Bush

Sand on the broad path before me whirled in circles as the wind picked it up. With a tremendous desire to worship the Father on one of heaven's mountains, I walked over unusually barren land toward Mt. Seraphim.

Camelia had desired to come with me and with the Father's blessings we had set out with her riding on my shoulder.

"It'll be a hard climb," I told her. She chirped, looking to the top of the mountain.

"Please give me the endurance I need, Father." He answered my prayer and we soon reached the top.

We rested under a large bush. There was no bright sun to hide from—the Father is the light in heaven—but the habits of earth were still ingrained in me.

Elation welled up in my soul as I looked out over heaven. "Praise be to God the Father," I sang. "Through Jesus He has created all things." Camelia chirped her own song of praise.

"I see I am not alone," someone said from behind the bush we sat under. A tall, princely man came around to meet us.

"We weren't aware anyone was here," I told him. "I hope

we didn't disturb you."

"The fact that you are here is no accident," he said. "The Father has a purpose in this." He spoke so confidently that I couldn't help but stare at him. "Have you come to burn in the fire, as I have?"

I must have looked as baffled as I felt. He appeared to realize I didn't understand and sat down beside me. He looked out over heaven with us.

"It is magnificent!" he observed.

"I was just quoting a psalm of praise," I told him, regarding him closely again. He gave me the impression that he was accustomed to having control. Somehow Camelia and I had happened upon his mountain and he wasn't sure what to do about it.

"The Father has appointed me commissioner over sectors of heaven and earth," he said. "At times it seems as though all creation wants to consult me. When I come here, the Father lifts the burden." He looked at me and asked, "Why have you come to the mountain?"

Camelia chirped a response that brought a smile to his face.

I told him, "I came because I had a tremendous desire to worship the Father on one of heaven's mountains."

"I have often felt a similar desire," he confessed, "but duty has kept me at my post. The Father has never convicted me of wrongly staying at my duty. But perhaps, if I gave deference to the desire to worship, I would not come under such heavy burdens."

Lightning ripped the sky and struck the bush we sat under. Flames instantly shot up from it. Acting instinctively, I scurried out from beneath its branches.

When I looked back, I saw the man and Camelia inside the blazing fire praising God. The bush continued to burn, but it was not consumed. *Just like the burning bush in the Bible,* I thought. There was a worshipful glow on the man's face. Looking at him, I longed to be in the fire.

"Step in, My daughter," the Father said.

The fire raged by this time. Trusting and praising the Father, I entered it.

How long we were in the fire, I don't know. I do know that when it finished burning I felt a new freedom from many of the earthly feelings and perceptions that had lingered with me.

When the man looked at me again, I could see that tears had washed his eyes. Glory radiated from his face. "Our God is a consuming fire!" he breathed. "Now I am ready to continue the work He has called me to do."

Camelia had not said a peep since the fire. He picked her up and placed her gently in my hands. "She'll need some rest." With that he turned and began his trek down the mountain.

"What is your name?" I called after him.

"I am David, son of Jesse."

Chapter 17 -- Miriam's Dance

She did turns and leaps across the studio floor. Elaine's daughter, Char, had come home. Having just been told that Miriam's dance would be performed at the Passover Celebration, she'd responded in dance, typical of her and Elaine.

Heaven would soon celebrate the Passover, and dance would be an integral part of the festivities. While Elaine showed Ruth and Lucian some Jewish steps, Char's attention returned to the small children she had been teaching to worship the Father through dance.

"You'll have to go slower. I can't follow you," Sara whined.

"I'll show you," Daniel said with his chest sticking out. Before Char stopped twirling, he did a few quick steps and tripped and fell.

"Are you all right?" Char asked helping him up.

"You can't get hurt in heaven," he muttered.

"Pride comes before a fall," Sara taunted.

Daniel's lip turned out in a pout.

"And love covers everything in heaven," I told them both. They lowered their heads.

Char smiled and said, "This is going to be the most marvelous dance. You're all doing so well."

All was quickly forgiven and they were soon back at learning their steps.

Trumpets electrified the air signaling the commencement of the ceremony.

"It's time to head for the sea!" Ruth shouted.

Everyone was excited. For many, this was their first Passover Celebration. We had already eaten the traditional meal of unleavened bread with bitter herbs and wine. Roasted lamb had not been a part of the meal because lambs are not sacrificed in heaven. After all, we were celebrating the Lamb of God who'd been sacrificed once and for all.

Upon leaving Elaine's home we found the pathways streaming with people headed for the sea. Joy saturated the air as children laughed and ran and adults talked excitedly.

Millions of people already lined the shore when we arrived. We were just in time to see Jesus raise His hands to the Father while Moses knelt at Jesus' feet, head bowed.

We watched in amazement as a strong wind from the Holy Spirit blew across the sea and divided the waters.

"Will I ever tire of this?" I asked the Father.

"Never."

Jesus stepped forward onto dry ground with walls of water on the right and left. We followed Him through the sea. The celebration dance would begin when we reached the other side.

Moses began to sing:

I will sing to the Lord, for He is highly exalted.
The horse and its rider He has hurled into the sea.

I looked up at the walls of water and a shiver went through my body. "How terrible it must have been for that army," I said to a woman walking beside me. She looked at the water and quickened her steps.

Daniel walked over to me and grabbed my hand. "I'm not afraid," he said, squeezing my hand.

"I know you're not, Dear."

When everyone reached the other side, Moses' sister Miriam picked up a tambourine and began a song and dance. Women with tambourines joined her, raising them above their heads. Others raised their hands or flags.

Char and the children danced with all their hearts. Elaine and the girls joined a Jewish folk dance. I observed silently, praising the Father in ecstasy.

Jesus watched the festivities with eyes filled with love for each brother and sister. A small child approached Him and tugged on His hand. "Dance with me, Jesus."

He picked her up and twirled her around. I could hear her laughing. Without breaking His step, He kissed her cheek, put her down and with a twirl picked up the next waiting child.

Daniel took my hand and delightfully we lost ourselves in the crowd, two-stepping to the music.

Chapter 18 -- City of Our God

After the celebration, all of heaven remained quiet for a season. I sat on my veranda enjoying the honeysuckle climbing its pillars. Its white flowers permeated the air with fragrant perfume. "All creation praises You, Father," I said looking beyond the honeysuckle toward the Mount of Worship.

Looking again at the flowers, I thought of the upcoming trip that Mother, Elaine, Char and I planned to take to the City of Our God. Each of us had a special reason for wanting to visit the city.

I turned and looked through the window at my crown, temporarily placed on my dining table. Camelia lay still in her nest. "It's a good thing you're still sleeping, dear Camelia." I spoke quietly so as not to wake her. "We have a long journey to make."

The doorbell clarioned an announcement. Without waking, Camelia buried her head under her wing.

"I'm on the veranda," I called, straining to see around the corner of the house. Elaine and Char came around to the veranda.

"Char is anxiously looking forward to our jaunt," Elaine told me as if we had been in mid-conversation. She said to Char, "You'll be absolutely amazed at the city; words can't describe it."

"Does it really have streets of gold?"

"The whole city is pure gold," I promised her, "gold transparent as glass."

Camelia woke at the sound of our voices and flew to my shoulder. She chirped loudly, telling us all about the city, I guess. She was so excited that we had to laugh.

Char encouraged her: "Camelia, you'll have to show us all the things you're telling us about," That was all Camelia needed; she was gone in a flash.

"We'd better get going," I advised, "Camelia could be there and back before we get started."

We stopped by Mother's home on the way. She and Martha were waiting for us by the footbridge, Martha saddled with an abundant basket of flowers.

"Now don't go so fast that you lose the flowers," Mother admonished her. Martha just brayed.

Skirting small villages, we followed the Sacred River through the countryside. Near the end of our journey we climbed a steep hill beside the river. There below us stood the City of Our God, laid out and bedecked like a bridal garment. The splendor of it took our breath away. The whole city shone like a brilliant jewel. "Oh, Father," I breathed, "its beauty never fails to bless me."

A breeze of the Holy Spirit picked us up and set us at the gate of the city.

Char was beside herself. She mumbled, "I can't believe all this!"

Just inside the city gate a huge trading center welcomed us. We would trade our flowers for items we desired. We each grabbed some flowers.

Mother and Martha set out to meet an old friend while Elaine and Char sought small rewards for each of Char's dance worship students. I scrutinized the shops along the widest street adjoining the gateway plaza and spotted the book trade center.

When I entered the massive shop, I was at first taken back by rows and rows of endless shelves of books. I followed overhead signs to the section called "Earth Issues." On a table with a "New Releases" sign, I found what I had come to the city for—a book written by my son, Travis.

"It's a very inspirational book," the woman behind the

table told me with a smile. "It will truly bless you."

"The sheer fact that it's here blesses me," I replied. She didn't understand, but she gladly took my flowers. I happily went off to read my book.

Camelia settled on my head. "So, you've found me, Dear. Look what I have here. My son wrote this." I showed her the book then gingerly opened its cover and began to read.

I hadn't read long before tears welled up in my eyes. "Things are getting very bad on earth," I told Camelia. She jetted away. I didn't pay much attention and went back to reading.

After a few more agonizing pages, I heard someone ask, "Has the whole world gone mad?" I looked up to see Jesus sitting beside me—Camelia perched on His shoulder. I stared at Him, numb. He motioned for the book; I handed it to Him.

"What do you perceive when you read of the happenings on earth? Do you see the problems as insurmountable, or do you see them as opportunities for the Father's power and glory to be displayed?"

I just stared at Him.

His eyes searched deep into my spirit. Faith radiated with His gaze into my soul.

"Though the hills be leveled and the mountains be removed, I will still praise Thee," I vowed.

He smiled and took my hand. "I have your son in My hand." His words filled me with faith and joy.

"Thank You, Jesus."

He handed the book back to me and rose to leave. As He walked toward the mount, Camelia flew back and alighted on the book's cover.

"Thank you, Camelia."

She chirped twice—her "You're welcome," I guess.

Chapter 19 -- The Boat Ride

Ruth and Lucian waited on the front steps of my home while Gina's friends, John and Heidi, walked up the footpath. We were all going on a picnic near the Golden Sea. When I opened the front door, the girls, spotted Camelia on my shoulder and promptly made a fuss over her.

"We're so glad you're coming with us," Ruth cooed. "We brought some special seeds for you." She took a bag of seeds out of her basket while Camelia danced on my shoulder.

"You found your way into her heart," I congratulated her.

Heidi was very quiet while we walked to the sea. I was about to ask her if she was okay when John said, "I've seen boats on the sea. I used to fish with my dad. Do you suppose someone might take us out in one?"

I smiled and told him, "We'll ask the Father."

When we reached the shore, a wind from the Spirit blew mist from the sea on us until we were drenched. We trembled under the Holy Spirit's power until the wind ceased.

"The boat is ready, if you care to go," someone yelled from down the shoreline. A man stood near a large fishing boat moored to some rocks. He hollered, "The Father said you would like to sail in my boat."

"Yes, we certainly would," Ruth yelled back. She ran toward the boat and was almost there when she realized she'd left her basket. She stopped and looked back. "My basket! Would someone please bring it." John picked it up and grabbed Heidi's hand to bring her along to the craft.

Our captain introduced himself with a pleasant smile. "My name is Andrew."

We introduced ourselves.

"We shall have a great excursion on the sea," he promised as he helped us board.

"I wonder if he's Peter's brother," Lucian whispered to me.

Andrew turned and said, "Yes, I am Peter's brother. And, no, Peter does not have keys to the gate of heaven." We all laughed.

The sea was breathtaking. We were all in a state of absolute bliss—all except Heidi. I noticed Andrew watching her. "Dear Father, what can she be thinking?" I asked.

She spoke to Andrew. "Do you know how I feel?"

"Yes, the Father has shown me. But tell me anyway."

"I feel like this is all a dream. Everything is so beautiful; everyone is so loving and kind. I feel like it can't be real. The only genuine happiness I experienced on earth was when I received Jesus into my heart. I felt His love and peace. But the world around me was still ugly and cruel. I'm not sure I can adapt here."

Andrew's response came slowly, with a sigh. "I had similar feelings when I followed Jesus on earth. My brother, Peter, and John and James all had such great moral strength. They understood Jesus. I, on the other hand, was so caught up in myself that I didn't have an inkling of how Jesus wanted to use me. Consequently, I didn't get close enough to enjoy Him."

"So what did you do?"

Andrew thought for a moment. "I went fishing."

That shocked us all.

"You went fishing?" Heidi repeated.

"Yes, I went fishing." He smiled. "I went fishing for men. I became interested in what Jesus was interested in. He was busy fishing for men, so I got busy fishing for men too. I got so busy that before I knew it I was marveling at what good friends we'd become. I immensely enjoyed His company."

Heidi looked confused.

Andrew expounded: "The preacher who told you and John about Jesus was fishing for men—sharing his friend Jesus with you." He paused to let his words sink in. "You need to let Jesus' joy and peace flow through you to others, Heidi."

We sailed on in silence for several knots. Then I heard Heidi telling Ruth and Lucian, "I have a beautiful piano in my home. If you'd like to learn to play, I'll teach you."

The girls giggled with delight.

"Thank You, Father," I said quietly.

Andrew had a sparkle in his eye.

Chapter 20 — Camelia's New Friend

She flew in through the window right behind Camelia and landed on the shelf by my crown. I'm sure Camelia's new friend, Alice, thought Camelia's nest was the most beautiful she'd ever seen. I stopped counting how many times Camelia brought her in to inspect it.

I so enjoyed my bird friends; their singing filled my heart with joy. Camelia had been singing more than ever lately.

"Your friend Alice may build a nest in my home, if she would like," I told her. She did a little jig on the shelf. She and Alice searched every corner of my home, but couldn't find a suitable niche. I requested the Father's help for their hunt.

The Father had given me a mission earlier and I had

been resting in preparation. It was now time to go. I took a gold ribbon from my drawer and tied it tightly around my hair. "I'll be back soon," I told Camelia. She flew a few circles around my head eyeing the gold ribbon before she and Alice flew out the window.

My mission went very well, though I was gone longer than I expected. When I returned, I wanted to relax. I loosened the ribbon from my hair and went to put it in its drawer. I found the drawer open. *I must have left it that way.*

"Oh my!" Among my gold ribbons was an elegant little nest. "Camelia! Alice can't make her nest in my ribbon drawer!" As usual, Camelia knew when to be gone. "They'll have to find another place," I said out loud to myself.

Camelia and Alice flew in through the window with grass in their beaks. They flew to the drawer and busily weaved the grass into the nest, chirping boisterously as they worked.

"Dear Father, I did tell them she could build a nest in my home, but now I see that I should have discussed it with You first. I really don't want her nest in my ribbon drawer. What should I do?"

"Hold out your hand." I held it out.
"Now look at it." I looked and in the palm of my hand was a golden seed.

He instructed me: "Plant the seed about five feet from your window and water it with water from the Sacred River."

I fetched a garden tool and went outside. Camelia and Alice flew to the window to see what I was doing. Five feet from my study window, I dug a hole and planted the seed. Then I went back into the house for a pitcher before starting down the path to the Sacred River. Camelia and Alice followed me, chirping impetuously. They sensed that something exciting was about to happen.

Having returned with the water, I poured it over the buried seed. Immediately, a golden plant began to grow. It grew and grew until it became a small tree. Its leaves and branches were of pure gold and glowed radiantly in the light. We stared at it in awe.

"Now take the nests," the Father directed, "and put them each on a branch."

Camelia and Alice watched me remove their nests from my crown and my drawer. I placed them near the center of the tree, each on its own branch.

Neither bird made a peep or moved a feather. They stood transfixed in awe of the tree. Then the leaves of the tree began to move as a breeze of the Holy Spirit blew through the branches into my window. The birds shivered with delight and sang. They flew to their nests and nestled in, quietly bowing their heads in praise.

"No problem is too insignificant for You, Father," I sighed. "Thank You."

Later, while resting on my window seat, I listened to my bird friends sing and watched them rejoice in their new home. I was reminded of the tree on the way to Ruth's cottage with all the gold ribbons.

"Father, You have answered the desire of Camelia's heart!"

"Yes," He said.

Chapter 21 -- Martha's Trouble

"Have you heard the news?" Mother asked excitedly.
"What news?"

She apologized, "Oh, please come in. I'm so emotional about this that I forgot my manners."

"Please tell me."

"Guess who Jesus asked to carry Him in the Palm Sunday procession."

"Martha?"

"Yes! Isn't it wonderful!" She was so ecstatic that she could hardly contain herself. She couldn't wait to tell me the whole story. She forgot all about asking me to sit down or offering me something to drink.

When she finished, I asked, "Is Martha as excited about it as you?"

"Is she excited?! She's stepped on so many flowers promenading around the gardens that it's lucky for her this is heaven and the flowers bounce right back up. She's had an endless line of donkeys coming to congratulate her. It really is an honor!"

"Oh, I'm so happy for her! Let's walk out to the gardens. I'd like to congratulate her as well. I'd also like to enjoy the gardens."

"Since the last visiting donkey left, I haven't heard a sound out of her," Mother reflected. "I suppose her visitors wore her out."

We walked out to the gardens and saw Martha lying under an evergreen tree near a small plot of lilies of the valley. "I guess she's sleeping," Mother said quietly. "You'll have to speak with her later."

"Oh my . . . oh my . . . oh my!"

"Someone is moaning," I said.

Martha let out a pitiful groan.

"That's Martha." Mother hurried over to her. With her hands on her hips, she looked down at her and forewarned, "This better not be one of your tricks, Martha."

"This is no trick. I'm trying so hard to be humble about all this that it's killing me."

I turned away to hide my laugh.

"Don't be foolish, Martha," Mother chided her. "Jesus considers you the best donkey, or He wouldn't have chosen you."

Martha groaned and rolled over.

"All you need is some rest. You've worn yourself out. After you've rested you'll see what a great honor this is and realize it's okay to be proud."

With that, Martha let out a loud bray.

"We'll leave you alone to rest," were Mother's parting words to miserable Martha before turning and starting back. She motioned for me to join her.

"Dear Father, Martha needs Your grace," I prayed.

"Grace is coming."

Reassured, I walked with Mother back to the house.

"Martha, what are you doing?" Jesus asked.

Martha looked up to find Jesus standing over her.

"It was a mistake to ask me to be your donkey for the procession."

"I don't make mistakes."

"But I've been so proud about all this," she moaned.

"And what did you do when you realized you were being proud?"

"I lay down to die to self."

Jesus looked at Martha lovingly. "Martha, of all the donkeys in heaven, I asked you to carry me because you had the most need of humility."

Martha looked at Jesus for a long moment. Then she brayed a laugh. "Does anyone else know this?"

"I've told only you," Jesus assured her.

"Good, let's keep it between us."

"Martha, Martha, you have a little more dying to self to do." Jesus hugged her and then left the garden.

While Mother and I conversed at her dining table, she said, "I thought I heard Martha laughing. She must be okay now."

Looking out the kitchen window I caught a glimpse of Jesus leaving the gardens.

I said, "Yes, she's fine."

Chapter 22 -- A Son is Home

Have I ever known a more intense feeling in heaven? Struggling with my emotions, I prepared his room. He would stay with me for a while.

Looking over the room, I thought about how long it had been since I had seen him. *What will he look like?* "Oh Father, how much longer? I've waited so long!"

"Very soon, my daughter."

Tears came to my eyes. The last news Jesus had told me about one of my sons was that he was working in a degenerate area of his city and the power of the Holy Spirit was flowing through him mightily. Many sinners were being saved through his preaching.

"He's here," the Father said. "Go to him."

Immediately I stood at the place of entry and saw Jesus hugging a man. Tears flowed freely from my eyes. I had loved him deeply on earth, but our spirits had never been united. Now we would be as one. As I watched him, my heart was knit to my son's heart.

When Jesus was about to leave, He motioned for me to come. I could see that my son was weeping as I approached.

"Mother!"

We fell into each other's arms and embraced for a long while. "Welcome home, Son."

"It's good to be home."

With tears flowing, he looked around heaven.

"You will stay with me for a while," I told him, "until Jesus completes your house." He nodded.

On our walk home he stopped often to admire the beautiful gardens and richly colored flowers lining our path. His tears relentlessly fell. I decided to take him to the Sacred River.

At the river I said, "Drink from the river, Son. It flows straight from the Throne Room with the Father's healing power."

He knelt and dipped his cupped hands into the water. As soon as he drank, his tears stopped flowing and a joyful expression broke over his face. A breeze of the Holy Spirit swept over him and he raised his eyes toward the Mount of Worship to praise the Father.

When he looked back at me he said again, "It's good to be home."

He told me about his mission on earth. I marveled at the work the Father had performed through him. It was a short work, but oh so powerful!

Angels greeted us with joyful songs when I opened my front door. My son mingled his voice with theirs and the glory of the Father surrounded us. We gratefully knelt in worship.

The Father reminded me of Scripture:

What do you think? If a man owns a hundred sheep and one of them wanders away, will he not leave the ninety-nine on the hills and go to look for the one that wandered off? And if he finds it, I tell you the truth: he is happier about that one sheep than about the ninety-nine that did not wander. In the same way, I tell you there is rejoicing in the presence of the angels of God over one sinner who repents.

Eventually, the angels left and I showed my son around my home. He caught his breath when he spotted the golden tree through my study window.

"It's so beautiful! And right outside your window!"

Camelia chirped a welcome from her nest.

"Oh Father! You have answered the desire of my heart

too!"

Chapter 23 -- The Messenger

Daniel and I were skipping stones across a small river when Little Sara came running and waving her arms frantically.

"Sara, dear, what's the matter?" She was always so dramatic. I usually found it humorous, but sometimes it was so overdone that it was annoying—like now.

"I have to stop and breathe!" She puffed emphatically. "I ran so fast! You have no idea what news I have."

Camelia and Sara had stretched my patience immensely, but looking down at Sara, I wondered if it had been enough.

Daniel put his hands on his hips. "Tell us, Sara."

Before she could tell us her news, a trumpet caroled in the distance.

"We need to go to the tabernacle," I told them.

"That's what I was going to tell you," Sara pouted. She stomped her feet.

We headed for the Tent of Meeting at the foot of the Mount of Worship. Men, women and children gathered under a sky already filled with angels.

A short, balding man stood behind a podium in the outer courtyard. "That's the Apostle Paul," Sara told us. I wondered how she knew what was happening before the rest of us.

"I tell her because she asks Me," the Father informed me.

"Oh."

I stared at Paul while he smiled at the massive crowd with joy blazing on his features. Restraining his excitement, he shouted, "There will be a great ingathering." Cheers erupted. He motioned for quiet. "We must prepare. Builders, artisans and especially carpenters will need extra help. Your brothers and sisters coming home may stay in your homes until theirs are finished."

"It's the rapture, isn't it?" Daniel whispered to me.

I was stunned, but managed to answer, "Yes."

"Soon," Paul went on, "you will be taken to the clouds. Many of you will meet your loved ones who are still on earth."

A long moment of silence followed. Then people started shouting praises to the Father. Some cried, some laughed, others—like me—were too overwhelmed to do anything.

Heaven was about to become a bustle of activity. My son's home had been finished; now he would help build his brothers' homes. My husband's room and my stepdaughter Lisa's room needed only finishing touches. Mother would prepare rooms for my dad and siblings. Elaine would ready her home for her husband and son.

Back at home, Camelia didn't know how to handle all the commotion. She flew in and out through the window constantly—Alice right behind her. They flew in, circled the room, lighted on something to watch us for a moment and then flew back out. After about the twentieth time, I said, "You'll wear yourself out, Camelia. There must be something you and your bird friends can do for the ingathering."

I prayed to the Father and He reminded me of the tree with the gold ribbons.

"Camelia, remember your tree with all the gold ribbons? There's a custom on earth of tying ribbons around trees to welcome loved ones home."

Camelia bent her head from side to side while keeping her eyes on me. Alice did the same. Camelia then hopped on one foot, then the other. Alice hopped too, of course. When their antics were finished, they flew out the window.

It didn't seem long before Daniel came running down the path, yelling, "All the birds are carrying gold ribbons. They must be going to a parade or something." I laughed, but didn't say anything.

Looking over the rooms that would soon be occupied by loved ones, my eyes filled with tears. *I must control my emotions*, I thought, remembering how draining it had been when my son came home.

"Come and see what the birds are doing," Daniel cried. I went outside to see a gold ribbon tied around every tree near my home.

"Camelia, you are such a blessing," I shouted into the air.

As I turned to go inside, I noticed Sara peering around the corner of my house with a downcast expression. I wondered what performance we would get now. She walked over with head down and arms folded.

"I've come to apologize. The Father told me I've been very proud."

Daniel and I looked at each other.

"It's just that sometimes it's hard to know when I'm being proud," she went on, raising her head to look at us. "Lucky for me, though, the Father always tells me,"

Daniel and I smiled.

"Would you children like some sweet cakes?"

Chapter 24 -- Bells and Pomegranates

"I don't understand the significance of the bells and pomegranates," Mother commented.

"The high priest wore them on the hem of his robe when he entered the Holy of Holies," Elaine explained. "If the bells kept ringing while he walked around, the people knew he was all right. If the bells stopped ringing, they pulled him out by a rope attached to his waist or leg."

"Why would they pull him out?" Mother asked.

"Because he could have been overcome by God's power.

Or, if he had entered the Holy of Holies unworthily"—her eyes widened—"like without his sin offering or improperly washed or attired, he could have even been struck dead."

"You're teasing me," Mother laughed.

"I heard the same thing," I told her. "We can ask Moses' brother Aaron when we see him."

"Well, Martha isn't going into the Holy of Holies," she assured us.

"No," Elaine laughed. "She's only carrying the Holy of Holies."

"Mother," I said, as soothingly as I could, "In heaven, bells ring out peals of worship and praise; that's why we're sewing them on Martha's blanket."

Mother attached another pomegranate made of blue, purple and crimson yarn to the blanket. "Martha will look so marvelous wearing this blanket—to think she will actually carry Jesus!" Her eyes moistened.

"She's been quite calm since Jesus talked to her," I commented.

"Not at all like the usual Martha," Elaine added.

"Martha is a real piece of handiwork," Mother said sweetly.

"I guess we're all pieces of work to the Father," I thought out loud.

Just then, we heard a loud uproar outside. We looked out and were dumbfounded to see the trees near the gardens full of bunkeys.

Oh no! I thought. *What are they up to now?*

"What in heaven are they doing here?" Mother asked. "I've never seen them outside the jungle before."

The bunkeys jumped down from the trees and stood perfectly still around the perimeter of the gardens—glaring at Martha.

Martha glared back for what seemed like a long time. Then she bowed her head.

The bunkeys charged. They climbed on her back and pulled her ears and mane. Martha walked around the gardens giving several of them a ride.

Mother became very distraught. "We need to chase them away! Look at them pulling on her ears; they'll hurt her!" She started for the door.

I put my hand on her shoulder. "No, Mother. The Father is behind this."

She stopped, but walked to the window to watch anxiously. "If only they'd stop."

The bunkeys rode Martha to exhaustion. We thought they would never stop. When they finally left, Mother hurried out to Martha. "I have to see if she's okay."

Elaine and I followed. We could hear Martha praising the Father.

"Did the bunkeys hurt you?" Mother asked hugging her.

"Yes, they hurt me," Martha answered humbly. "They hurt my pride." She raised her head and fixed her eyes on the Mount of Worship.

The rest of us looked in time to see a brilliant shaft of light shine from the mountaintop into the garden. Jesus appeared before us in splendorous glory. We knelt in adoration.

"Are you ready Martha?" He asked.

"Yes."

We rose to our feet.

"Your blanket!" Mother cried. "You need your blanket!"

Elaine quickly ran to the house to fetch Martha's blanket. When she returned, Jesus placed it on Martha and then mounted her. They headed slowly toward the Mount of Worship. The rest of us ran ahead excitedly to cut palm branches.

Vast crowds lined the path ascending the mount. Everyone waved branches and shouted Hosanna when Jesus passed. "Blessed is He who comes in the name of the Lord!" they shouted. "Blessed is the King of Israel! Blessed is the King of Heaven!"

What unspeakable joy we felt. Even the angels sang more gloriously than usual. Jesus had gone to the cross and died

for all men after the first Palm Sunday, but this Palm
Sunday re-enactment would begin the Resurrection Celebration.

After the celebration, back at Mother's home, I recounted
everything that had happened to Martha and pondered
how the Father often causes circumstances that help to
keep us spiritually balanced. I thought about how the bells
on Martha's blanket had expressed the Holy Spirit's power
while the pomegranates had expressed His love. I contemplated, too, how the pomegranates had formed a cushion
between the bells to prevent them from clashing together.
They had allowed them to ring out a clear, harmonious,
beautifully balanced tone.

Mother said, "I guess Martha needed those bunkeys," and
thanked the Father for them.

Yes, the Father was changing us all.

Chapter 25 -- The Heavenly Rapture

The doorbell rang and my son went to open the door.
Elaine had come with an old friend who had recently
arrived in heaven. Clint hugged each warmly and invited
them in.

"So Lorraine, how do you like heaven?" I asked her as I
hugged her.

She choked back tears to say, "It's so wonderful! It's
beyond description! She looked at Elaine. "It's not fair that
Elaine got to come before I did." We all laughed.

"You've come at an exciting time," I said. "The great ingathering will be very soon."

"Is your home prepared for the rest of your family?" Clint asked her.

"This is all too much for me!" she sighed, and sat down.

"It's too much for all of us," Elaine acknowledged. "That's why the Father has told everyone to bathe in the Golden Sea. We need His anointing power to be able to stand in His presence during this time."

Clint raised his arm like a general leading his brigade and proclaimed, "To the sea we shall go!"

Camelia heard him say go from the courtyard and zipped through the window to perch on his shoulder.

"Isn't your friend coming?" Clint asked her. Before he finished asking, Alice lighted beside Camelia. Clint laughed. "Looks like we're all here. No, wait! Where are Char and Grandma?"

"They'll join us when we reach the forest," I told him. "They're so anxious to get there that it wouldn't surprise me if we find they went ahead without us."

The Spirit's sweet anointing saturated the air as we started down the path toward the sea. Lorraine had a hard time walking under the glory, so Elaine held her arm to steady her. No one said a word as we marched. Tears of joy rolled down our faces. Our thoughts were on the loved ones we would soon see. We stopped to rest occasionally—more to recoup our emotions than our strength.

While still on our way, a gentle breeze of the Spirit picked us up and floated us to the sea. It set us down on the shore in the midst of millions of people waiting to enter the water. Making their way slowly to the shoreline, some wept, others praised the Father.

When we reached the water, my son offered to help Lorraine. "Can you make it, or shall I help you?"

Lorraine just looked out over the water and wept. Clint took her arm and put it around his neck then helped her walk into the sea. The rest of us followed.

Waves of the Holy Spirit splashed on us, strengthening and invigorating us. Joy welled up and spilled over into laughter. Angels helped children splash and play in the sea's lagoons. Our heightened emotions washed away leaving only deep peace. Camelia and Alice sang and danced on our heads.

While floating in the sea, a Scripture came to mind: *We who are still alive will be caught up together with them, (those who have died) to meet the Lord in the air. And so we will be with the Lord forever.*

I thought about the monumental miracle that was about to take place, how Jesus' followers on earth would escape earth's time of tribulation.

"Why do you love us so much?" I asked the Father.

A wave of His Spirit enveloped me, allowing me to know more of His love.

"I think I could float in this sea forever," Clint said while floating past me. Soon, though, it was time to leave the water.

A breeze of the Spirit dried our robes as we stood on the shore. It left both our robes and our skin glimmering with a golden glow.

A powerful command ruptured the expanse between heaven and earth. Everyone trembled hearing the voice of the arch-angel thunder across the sky. The color drained from Lorraine's face as she stood motionless.

With no further delay, a shout went out from the Throne Room and the trumpet of the Father (a ram's horn called a shofar) sounded.

We found ourselves standing on earth—our graves open and empty. With wonderfully glorified bodies we met our earthly loved ones who had also been changed in the twinkling of an eye into glorious beings.

Crying for joy, we hugged and kissed. Hand in hand, arm in arm, husbands, wives, fathers, sons, mothers, daughters, brothers and sisters rose to meet Jesus in the air.

We could see Jesus in the clouds. His eyes glistened with

tears and His arms opened wide to receive us.

Our eyes fastened on Him. His love and glory surmounted all other existence. When we reached Him, He turned and led us triumphantly into heaven. There, He would welcome each individual member of His bride to our wedding feast.

Chapter 26 -- Charity and Vicky

Sitting quietly in the picturesque Valentine Garden, enjoying a refreshing time of fellowship with the Father, I looked over trees laden with red hearts. Just as Jesus had often retreated to the Garden of Olives while on earth, this had come to be my heavenly garden of repose.

So much had happened recently. The wedding feast had been beyond description. And now my home was filled with loved ones. *How restful to sit here in my celestial garden and visit with Daddy.* I often thought of the Father as "Daddy" during times of endearment.

Leaning back on the grass covered with tiny heart flowers, I whimsically picked one and held it to the sky. A ray of light shone on it and made it sparkle.

"I love you," it said.

Knowing that the Father had given the words, I smiled and said, "I love You too, Father." The flower sparkled brighter and danced in my hand. I laughed.

A breeze of the Holy Spirit swept over me, bringing to remembrance my first visit to this garden shortly after my arrival in heaven. I remembered how I had marveled at its beauty. Its babbling brook—I called it Kerith Brook—rambled peacefully beneath occasional ornamental footbridges. The luxurious, bright red glow of the valentines had been so intense that it almost blinded me. *Yet, none of this garden's beauty could compare to the majesty of Jesus on the Mount of Worship.*

I remembered the two valentines that had flown to earth. Their recipients, Charity and Vicky, were now in heaven. They were no longer girls but young women. Each had a lovely home close to other members of their family who lived near the City of Our God.

How funny it had been when they came to visit me after the ingathering. They never expected to find birds in my home—much less birds that perched on their heads and tried to take their ribbons.

The Father had later summoned Camelia and Alice and their friends to a retraining session. After their session, I could wear my gold ribbons again. I smiled at the thought.

I looked again at the small heart flower in my hand. Its petals opened wide to look back at me. I held it to the sky and said, "Please give this to Jesus for me, Father." The flower blazed with a brilliant luster and floated into the sky. I watched it glide toward the Mount of Worship. The sky above the mount shimmered with dazzling colors. I knew Jesus was resting with the Father. I lay my head back on a cushion of valentine grass and listened to angelic choirs singing in the heavens. I closed my eyes to sleep.

Chapter 27 — Jesus the King

My husband asked the Father if he and I could watch the armies of heaven prepare for the great battle. With the Father's approval we walked hand in hand to the battle training fields at the farthest corner of heaven. We sat on a hill overlooking a site where Joshua and other great military leaders instructed a large number of generals.

Warrior angels amazed us with their strength and power as they demonstrated fighting techniques. The horsemen of heaven instructed charioteers.

My husband viewed the maneuvers with keen interest, but I had little taste for war, and mixed feelings about the coming battle.

"It is necessary for it to be this way," the Father told me. "I am a God of love, but I cannot love in truth without justice."

Meditating on His words, I thought, "*Yes, I can see how love without justice would produce chaos.*"

A large herd of galloping white steeds approached the fields. "*They are so beautiful! How awesome the cavalcade of heaven will look descending to earth.*"

My sons were on the fields preparing along with millions of others. They were also being trained to be officials on earth after the battle. Jesus, of necessity, would rule with an iron rod.

"I wonder what I will do on earth," my husband mused.

The Father told him, "There is much for you to do right now in heaven."

It was time to get back to our duties. The affairs of heaven carried on as usual in spite of an influx of new believers. Their stories of recent happenings on earth were horrendous. We all took solace in knowing that the Father would soon establish righteousness and justice on earth through Jesus.

During heaven's preparation for the battle, a well known

chorus became everyone's favorite. Its words and melody were presently lodged in my mind:

The Lamb will overcome the wicked
Because He is Lord of Lords and King of Kings.
With Him will be His called, chosen and faithful.

I hungered and thirsted for Jesus' return to earth to stop all the wickedness and violence. I longed so much for the Father to be glorified on earth rather than defied.

As we walked home, I realized that we hadn't seen Camelia on the training fields. She had been spending her time there lately. Mother had sewn a little coat of armor for her. Camelia didn't need it for protection, of course, but she looked so cute in it.

Dad had gotten someone to help Mother with her flowers while he and Martha carried water from the Sacred River to the fields. Martha and Dad had become very good friends.

Arman spent much of his time working with the charioteers. He loved the anticipation of battle. When they weren't working, the horses of fire watched the exercises from the surrounding hills. Their presence caused the hills to radiate.

Not long after my husband's and my visit to the battle training fields, Elaine and I were instructing some newly arrived Christians in God's Word when the heavens were suddenly shattered by a trumpet blast. The armies of the world had gathered in the Valley of Jehoshaphat to fight against Israel.

The trumpet sounded again. No one spoke while the residents of heaven assembled on the military fields. Soldiers' robes of pure, fine linen glowed whiter than snow. Mounted on their white horses, the armies passed in review before the Father under the command of Jesus.

Jesus rode majestically on His white horse. The Father had written a name on Him that He alone knew. Multiple crowns rested on His head. His eyes blazed fire; His robe dripped blood. A sharp two-edged sword projected out of His mouth to strike down the armies of earth. Written on His robe and on His thigh were the words "King of Kings and Lord of Lords." Everyone bowed to the ground as He passed.

I was astounded to see Jesus' face full of wrath. I trembled, feeling a sharp pain of sorrow pierce my heart. "Oh Father! Jesus isn't like the brother I know and love. I don't know this fierce man!"

The Father commanded, "Look at My Son, daughter! I am well pleased with Him."

I lifted my head just as He passed. He looked straight ahead, facing the coming battle with great purpose. Then, I saw a tear fall from the corner of His eye and I remembered how He had wept over Jerusalem.

I heard a chirping sound. *"Oh! There's Camelia!"* She was perched on His shoulder, wearing her little coat of armor.

Everyone began to shout, "Hallelujah! Salvation, glory and power belong to our God, for true and just are His judgments! Our Lord God Almighty reigns! Rejoice and be glad and give Him glory!" The anointing of the Holy Spirit flooded my heart and I rejoiced with all my strength.

"Save My people, Israel!" The Father thundered.

Uncountable armies cheered as they rode out of heaven into the clouds. When they were lost to our sight, the golden light of heaven deepened, bathing everyone in the Father's glory. Spontaneous songs of praise ascended unto the Father.

By and by, the songs ended, but no one went home. Everyone waited for word from the battle. I raised my hands in praise to the Father. They no sooner went up than I felt something in the palm of my right hand. It was a little valentine flower. Its tiny petals opened wide to look at me. I closed my hand gently over it and held it to my heart.

"I love You, Jesus."

When the battle would be over and Jesus' reign as King

on earth would begin, the lives of the citizens of heaven would change. There would be stories of heaven and earth.

The Land of Heaven

Part Two

Stories of Heaven and Earth

Chapter 28 -- He is the King

"It seems like an eternity," I said to myself while waiting for news from the battle. I smiled when I realized what I had said. *I'll express my feelings in heavenly terms eventually.* Looking around, I was relieved that no one appeared to have heard me.

I heard a soft laugh. "Oh Father, please forgive me," I breathed. "I didn't mean to be proud; I'm just so overwhelmed by this battle."

Before the Father responded, the loud blast of a trumpet broke the expectant calm over heaven. Heaven's golden light began to refract in the way it would when passing through a prism. A magnificent array of colors surrounded us. We fell to our knees under the Holy Spirit's anointing power. Then the Father's thunderous voice filled the expanse of heaven: "My Son reigns as King on earth!"

Each person reacted in his or her own way to the Father's joyous news. Some rose to dance; others remained kneeling. Some shouted hallelujah while others sobbed. I cried while raising my hands in praise.

The angels began a victory song and some of us started waving flags and marching. Those kneeling worshipped and offered praise. Eventually, everyone joined in the angels' refrain:

Great is the Lord and most worthy of all praise
In the City of Our God, the city of the great King.

"Oh Father! How can I thank You enough? Jesus is King at last!" I looked toward the east for Jesus' return.

My mother drew near and whispered, "Will Jesus return to heaven before He begins His reign?" Before I could explain, we heard a thunder of hoofbeats above the songs of praise.

My husband yelled, "Look! They're coming!"

What a glorious sight! When they drew nearer I could see that Jesus' face was no longer full of wrath. It manifested a radiant look of victory. His robe that had been covered with blood before the battle now glimmered white. Everyone stepped back to allow Him and the returning armies to pass. The multitudes of heaven cheered and waved palm branches as He passed.

Jesus had never looked so glorious. Looking straight ahead, His eyes shone with deep love for the Father as He eagerly approached the Mount of Worship.

"Hallelujah to the King!" we shouted.

I spotted Camelia, still perched on Jesus' shoulder. She, too, looked straight ahead as they rode toward the mount.

When Jesus reached the Tent of Meeting at the foot of the mount, the Father spoke to the innumerable throng: "Every knee shall bow before My Son."

The armies dismounted, knelt and bowed to their King as Jesus' steed turned to face them. The rest of heaven then bent our knees in worship.

Looking up, we saw that Jesus wore an expression of gratitude. He said, "Thank you for glorifying My Father." His loving gaze transfixed our souls. Our spirits merged into oneness. All of heaven was muted by the experience.

Jesus then turned and proceeded up the Mount of Worship. Everyone remained kneeling and watched Him ride to the summit. He was lost to our sight when a cloud covered the mountaintop. The cloud soon filled with a multitude of colors.

Elaine, with a dazzled look about her, leaned toward me and whispered, "Jesus is basking in the love of the Father."

I was so emotional that I was barely able to respond. "Isn't it wonderful!"

The celebration excelled all around us. We knew that Jesus would join us later. Not one person would miss His appreciative embrace. Singing and dancing surrounded the armies. Saints put wreaths of flowers on the necks of warrior horses and crowns of flowers on soldiers' heads.

"I didn't think I'd have enough flowers for all these wreaths," Mother said. "I believe Jesus multiplied them." She smiled brightly.

"They're beautiful!"

I placed a crown of flowers on a soldier's head and gave her a hug. She smiled thanks through tears of joy.

While taking in all that I could of the celebration, I noticed my husband questioning some soldiers about the battle. I refrained from joining him, not wanting to hear all the gory details. Jesus had won; that was enough for me.

Feeling exhausted by all the excitement, and the pure joy, I searched for a solitary spot and found one beside a row of balsam trees. I sat and buried my face in my hands to commune with the Holy Spirit.

Camelia lighted on my shoulder and tried to kiss my cheek. I removed my hands from my face and smiled at her, then stroked her tiny feathered head with my finger. "I'm glad you're home Camelia."

She looked at me lovingly then nestled in the flow of my hair. We closed our eyes and savored the sounds of the celebration.

Chapter 29 -- Family Meeting

I searched my loved ones' faces. We were gathered around my dining table talking and laughing, excited about the upcoming events. My mind drifted back to the many times I'd dreamed of the day they'd all serve the Lord wholeheartedly. Now, here we all sat full of joy, anticipating our new roles in the Kingdom of God.

My husband's face was serene, the worry lines gone from his forehead. David's expression displayed great determination. His driving desire to join the work already in progress was detectable in his eyes. Clint wore a look of total submission. Emptied of self, he waited on the Lord. Travis laughed enthusiastically at the turn of events, eager to take his part in the work. Lisa calculated every comment to verify that all was said and done in truth and righteousness.

With tear-filled eyes, I spoke to the Father: "Father, You have answered every prayer, every desire of my heart." My family was too deep in conversation to notice my prayer.

"Cleanup will be the first priority," David said, as though taking a strong stance.

"Many people are wounded or burned, so a massive healing program will come first," my husband refuted in his matter-of-fact tone. "Soldiers are already working with the sick and wounded."

Though earth was truly a mess, we were all sure that God had everything under control. Discussing it was merely a vent for our excitement.

Clint said, "Things will miraculously improve when water from the temple in Jerusalem begins to flow through the land. Think of it: health care and insurance will be things of the past!" We all stopped and thought about it.

"Earth will again become a Garden of Eden," I said. "No sickness. No disease." Aware of what it currently looked like, it was difficult for us to imagine.

"I need to go to a training meeting," Travis said. "Anyway, we'll have a better idea of what the Father's plans are after we've heard from Jesus."

Before he left, we bowed our heads and my husband spoke to the Father: "Father, we thank You for making us a part of this momentous undertaking. Thank You for the lordship and kingship of Your Son, Jesus. Glorify Him and Yourself in all we put our hands to."

We departed for our assigned work. I had been appointed to work with a group of women who would minister to Christians in my home state, Wisconsin.

I reflected on our discussion as I walked toward my place of training. For a season we would be restricted by earth's time. We'd be working on earth during earth's daylight hours and returning to heaven during earth's night hours. While in heaven, we'd be able to fellowship with friends and family.

Some of my friends, including Heidi and John and Ruth and Lucian, I would be able to see only at celebrations or special events. Heidi and John were assigned to a small city in England and Ruth and Lucian were already in northern Australia.

I will miss them, I thought, and began to grieve in my spirit. "Father, will I be so busy that I won't have time with You, either? And what about Jesus? When will I see Him?"

Tears welled up in my eyes.

The Holy Spirit swept over me with His peace. The Father said, "I am always with you. You will never be too busy for Me if it is in your heart not to be."

Jesus appeared and took my hand. Observing my tears, He said, "Have you forgotten that I am God and My Spirit can be in more than one place at a time? With My glorified body I will see you in heaven or on earth as the Father leads."

I smiled and hugged Him, confessing my foolishness. "I'm so glad You are God!"

Having put my mind at rest, He turned and walked away, greeting and hugging people as He passed them.

Things will be different now. I thought. But watching Jesus minister along His way, I realized some things would never change.

Chapter 30 -- The Earthly Mission

"My first mission to earth! My first mission to earth!" I was so excited I kept repeating it aloud to myself. I was a little afraid. I didn't want to see the evidences of atrocities and devastation that remained from the seven years of tribulation.

"I give my fears and apprehensions to You, Father. Please give me Your thoughts, feelings and emotions." His peace entered my spirit instantly.

Having filled my carry bag with necessary supplies, I

started walking the flower-lined path out to the gate where Elaine waited for me.

She shouted, "This is so exciting!"

"Yes it is!" I hollered back.

We were so eager that we arrived at the place of entry without much time to converse on our way. The women in our training group greeted us cheerfully. We were all anxious to start the much-needed work. We joined hands in pairs and closed our eyes. I felt the presence of the Holy Spirit engulf me before experiencing the sensation of being transported.

When I opened my eyes, I was standing at the door of a small, white house, still holding Elaine's hands. I stepped back and surveyed the house. Damaged from neglect and the violence of war, it was in much need of repair.

When I looked at Elaine, I was surprised at her attire. She donned a navy-blue, shirt-waisted dress with elbow-length sleeves. It buttoned in front with small, white buttons the entire length of the dress. White bands trimmed its sleeves and crew neck.

She stared back at my attire. I looked down and was given a start by my light-blue, paisley-print cotton skirt and white blouse with complementary embroidered light-blue butterfly collar.

"You look so different," Elaine said, suppressing a laugh. It definitely was a change from my glorious white robe. We both laughed.

"Well, we'd better get to work," I said.

Elaine knocked on the door. A long moment of silence followed before we heard something move inside. Then there was quiet again. She knocked again.

A timid, spiritless voice asked, "Who is it?"

"We're two sisters of mercy," Elaine answered. "May we help you?"

Staring at the closed door, we listened for a response. We heard a bolt being drawn back before the door opened slowly, just a crack. A portion of a small face peered through the opening.

"We have some food and medicine, if you're in need." Elaine held up her carry bag for the small person to see. The door opened wider to reveal a young girl whose eyes were fearful as she allowed us into the house.

She couldn't have been more than twelve years old. Tangled brown hair hung over her eyes. Her dress was torn and dirty. She had burns on her light-brown face and arms. My heart ached for her.

"Are you alone?" I asked, glancing around the room. I realized it was the wrong thing to ask when I saw her fear increase. I smiled lovingly to reassure her.

Her eyes filled with tears as she told us, chokingly, "My mother is in the back; she's sick." She pointed down a hallway.

"We have some food for you and your mother," I told her, "and some healing salve for your burns. May we see your mother?"

She led us through a dark hallway to a dim room in the back of the dwelling. The windows were boarded shut, as were all the windows in the house. The air was foul with the smell of sickness and decay.

I leaned over the woman and examined her emaciated face. Prematurely white hair stuck to her feverish brow. Her eyes were dark and sunken. She gathered all her strength to gasp, "In the name of Jesus, please help us!"

"That's why we're here," I told her.

Elaine opened her carry bag and took out a bottle of water. "Please drink some of this. It's sacred water from the Throne Room of heaven." The woman looked at her doubtfully, but reached for the water. I saw that it was difficult for her to hold the jar, so I braced her head up and helped her bring it to her lips. After she drank a little, I thought I noticed thin scale-like things fall from her eyes. As her eyes brightened, she breathed a sigh of relief.

Elaine started applying healing salve to the young girl's burns. "They're disappearing before my eyes!" the girl squealed in astonishment. Elaine smiled and continued applying the salve.

The mother sat up, although still weak from severe malnutrition.

"We have some bread we want you to eat." I told her. "It will satisfy your hunger for many weeks. It's food of angels." I hoped she was understanding me.

She started praising and glorifying God. "Praise You, Father! Thank You, Jesus! I knew You would help us!" She reached up and hugged me.

I took bread out of my bag and handed each a piece. I could see strength enter their bodies as they ate. They must have felt some kind of sensation because they looked at each other and started laughing. Elaine and I laughed with them.

"Now, on a serious note," I broke off, "I'm sure your water has been contaminated. We need to put some sacred water into your well to purify it. Where is your well?"

The girl showed us the opening to their well and we poured sacred water down. I told her, "You'll need to wash each item in your house with the pure water."

When we went back into the house, her mother was standing, smiling at us. "Nancy!" she exclaimed, "the Lord has sent His angels to lift us up—like the Bible says!"

"No, we're not angels," I corrected her. "We're humans like you, only glorified. After Jesus won the great battle, He sent us here to earth along with many other saints to help our fellow Christians."

"We're actually sisters," Elaine added with a warm smile. "That's why I told you we were sisters of mercy."

Though mother and daughter looked confused, we couldn't stay to explain everything.

"I see you have a Bible near your bed," I said. "Read the Book of Revelation; it will help you understand."

Reaching into my bag again, I pulled out a small sack of seeds. "Here are some seeds to plant. Water them with the purified water and in a few months you'll have delicious vegetables." I handed the seeds to the mother.

Elaine handed each a few small loaves of bread. "These will feed you until your vegetables are ready to eat."

"I'm sorry we must leave so soon," I told them, "but there are many people we must see today."

As we were leaving, the mother asked, "What are your names?"

I told her our names and she returned, "I'm Gretchen and this is my daughter Nancy." We all hugged.

"It has been a pleasure meeting you," I said sincerely.

"Thank you, angels," Nancy breathed sweetly. Her mother nodded. We smiled and waved goodbye as we walked out the door.

"Thank you and God bless you," Gretchen said.

Elaine and I chatted on our way back to our rendezvous with the others.

"They really thought we were angels." I chuckled. "Won't they be surprised the day they see a real angel."

"Angels do sometimes appear as humans," Elaine conceded. "But still, having seen the massive figures of Michael and Gabriel, the thought is hilarious."

We burst out laughing.

Chapter 31 -- Dead Flowers

Sometime after my first earthly mission, Mother asked me to visit her gardens with her. I was not prepared for what I saw. She showed me some flowers in her Victory Garden that she said were new. "Don't they look horrible!" she complained with a disgusted look.

I agreed. "If I didn't know better, I'd say they were dead." We were baffled, to say the least.

"They look dead, but they can't be," she said. "This is heaven! Jesus gave me these seeds and told me to plant them." She pointed to an empty bag near the flowers. Looking at the flowers as though she blamed them for their unattractiveness, she said, "These are what came up." She looked back at me. "Do you think Jesus got the seeds mixed up?"

"You think Jesus might have mixed up the seeds? That's preposterous!"

"He never makes mistakes," Martha agreed. We turned to look at her. "He told me so Himself." She then looked down at the blooms and after staring at them a moment admitted, "They're the ugliest flowers I've ever seen."

I had to admit she was right. They were a mottled yellowish brown, and worse than that, they gave off an awful odor.

"Stink, don't they," Martha observed.

I nodded. "Sure do. Maybe they're not flowers."

"What else could they be?" Mother sighed.

"Maybe they're some kind of herb for earth."

"From what I've heard, it smells like earth," Martha said innocently,

I smiled, "Yes, Martha, there are some bad smells on earth, but earth doesn't literally stink."

She gave me a look that plainly said, "What's the difference?"

I realized it was time to ask the Father about the new flowers. The Father, knowing what had transpired, said,

"The plants are herbs for healing. I think they look beautiful and have a pleasant scent."

We looked down at the plants, stupefied.

"If you'd like," the Father said, "you may plant the herbs in a garden separate from the flower gardens."

Mother's face brightened. "Yes, Father." She smiled her approval.

Still staring at the brown plants, I said, "After seeing earth, I know these herbs will be greatly appreciated. I guess it's difficult to know something's worth by just looking at it."

"Do you really think people will eat them?" Martha asked. "I can't imagine people getting them past their noses."

At that moment we heard a rumble like distant thunder. The Father spoke: "Go and get some sacred water from the creek."

We quickly carried buckets to the creek thinking that when we poured the creek water on the plants they'd become beautiful and smell like flowers—the way things are supposed to look and smell in heaven. I tremendously enjoyed watching the Father's miracles. We joyfully carried water back to the garden and waited for further instructions from the Father.

"Now, drink some of the water."

We were dumbfounded. Moreover, from the tone of the Father's voice, we didn't dare question. I dipped my hands into the water and drank. Mother followed suit. Then Martha stuck her head into the bucket and slurped up some water as well.

The Holy Spirit helped us understand how we had not recognized Him at work in the little plants. We repented with tear-filled eyes.

Mother lovingly moved closer to the herbs and said, "You may stay in my flower garden as long as you wish."

With moist eyes, I said, "I know you'll be very appreciated on earth, and I appreciate you too." The plants started to sway as though they were pleased.

"If anyone says you stink, or you look ugly, just tell me. I'll tend to them," Martha vowed.

A breeze of the Holy Spirit swept across the Victory Garden changing the plants to beautiful deep yellow with the fragrance of a rose. We looked on in amazement.

Have they actually changed, I wondered, *or are we seeing them with new eyes? Maybe their appearance changed because our hearts changed.*

We watched the herbs dance in the breeze of the Holy Spirit for a long while.

"Father, Your miracles are wonderful." I raised my hands in praise toward the Mount of Worship. "Even more wonderful are the miracles You perform in our hearts."

"Amen," said Mother and Martha.

Chapter 32 -- An Iron Skillet

When Jesus asked if I would go on a second earthly mission in the same vicinity as my first, I hoped conditions had improved. I was skeptical when Camelia asked to come along, but I soon learned that the company of a heavenly being is a rich blessing on earth.

After helping an elderly woman near the village where we'd begun our mission several weeks earlier, we rested a few moments beside a small, quiet stream. Our mission had brought us full circle.

"It's been a long day, Camelia," I sighed. She'd been

riding on my shoulder. She slanted her head to look at me; then she hopped over and snuggled up to my ear. We shut our eyes to the bright sunlight. The sun's heat baked the parched earth around us that had once been the bed of a large river. "It's definitely not the soft light of heaven," I said.

We knew Jesus was helping scientists and environmentalists to restore the atmosphere to its natural state. "Soon, the air will be pure and clean again," I consoled Camelia. She nodded then nestled further into my hair.

While we rested, the Father said, "When you're refreshed, would you visit Gretchen and Nancy before returning home."

"We'd love to, Father."

When we felt renewed, we began our short trip to Gretchen and Nancy's home. Camelia had heard a lot about the mother and daughter and was eager to meet them. She flew circles around my head as I walked.

"Camelia, I can't see where I'm going!" Politely, she perched again on my shoulder.

As we approached the village, I noticed the yards were much greener. Gretchen and Nancy's was the greenest. "What a tremendous difference the sacred water has made," I remarked to Camelia.

I hardly recognized their little house, painted shining white. Damaged siding had been replaced and the eaves troughs and windows had been repaired.

Camelia flew to a fruit tree in their yard and chirped a song. When I knocked on the door she flew back to me, not wanting to miss anything.

The door opened immediately this time. Nancy smiled at us excitedly. "Mom, one of the angels is here, and she has a bird with her!"

Camelia chirped a hello, at which Nancy giggled.

"Oh my!" Gretchen exclaimed. "We're so glad to see you. Please come in."

I stared at Gretchen. Clean and stylish in her crisp cotton

dress, she looked twenty years younger. Her hair was no longer white but brown. Her soft, light brown skin glowed.

Nancy was very pretty. Her bright red ribbon in her shiny brown hair and her red and white jumper both accentuated her rosy cheeks.

Gretchen pulled on my arm. "Please do come in."

"I didn't mean to stare. You both look so wonderful!"

"It's a true miracle!" Nancy declared, running her hands over her cheeks.

I looked around the kitchen and found it clean and tidy.

"You must have a taste of our fresh vegetables," Gretchen said, "These are from the seeds you gave us." She held out some vegetables in a bowl. "You eat vegetables, don't you?"

"Yes, of course." I reached for something that looked like a bean. Camelia settled on my hand as I selected the crisp pod. "Oh, this is my friend, Camelia." I lifted my hand higher.

"Is it an angel bird?" Nancy asked.

Camelia did her little tilting-the-head routine. Then she flapped her wings and chirped extra shrill.

"No, she's not an angel bird. I think what she's trying to say is that she can fly faster than any angel." While Gretchen and Nancy laughed, I realized I was beginning to understand Camelia.

I looked around their kitchen again. This time an iron skillet hanging on a wall near the oven caught my attention. It had an open Bible displayed in it. Gretchen smiled as she watched me ponder the crude shrine.

"I suppose that looks rather peculiar," she said. "The skillet belonged to my mother. She always used to tell me, 'God's Word is like that iron skillet: strong, sturdy and true. But, you wouldn't want to hit anyone over the head with it.' You can imagine what that skillet would do to someone's head."

"Yes," I replied, "and I can also imagine what the spirit looks like that's been hit by a loveless gospel. Your mother is a very wise woman."

"She died a few months before your first visit. Would you please give her a message." Her eyes moistened.

When Camelia saw tears forming in her eyes, she flew to her and chirped a soothing melody on her shoulder. Gretchen appreciatively smiled and petted her head. I thought Camelia was doing a wonderful job in her earthly ministry.

"Yes, I will give her your message, but I'm sure she'll be visiting you soon."

Nancy jumped up and down clapping her hands. "Grandma's coming to see us!"

"What's her name?" I asked.

Gretchen told me her mother's name and asked me to be sure to remember to pass along her message. I assured her I would.

Our mission almost over, I told mother and daughter that Camelia and I needed to leave.

Camelia flew to my shoulder.

"Will we see Jesus soon?" Nancy asked.

"Very soon," I said. Plans are being made for His coronation. I'll see that you're both present for it, Father willing."

I hugged each of them and Camelia gave each a kiss. They petted her head reciprocally. It seemed as though Camelia was becoming more affectionate.

As was my custom, after waving goodbye I reviewed our visit while walking down the road. I thought about the iron skillet. *What a wonderful lesson!*

Passing a small vegetable garden, I remembered the bean I had absentmindedly put in my pocket. I took it out and took a bite, then handed a small piece to Camelia.

"It's delicious!" I said.

"Of course," Camelia chirped.

Chapter 33 -- Time to Sow

I knew Elaine would be especially thrilled about a particular mission Jesus had given us. He allowed me to be the one to surprise her with it. I invited her to my home to share the news.

"We're going to Jerusalem," I told her.

"I knew it!" she gushed. "When do we leave?"

"Soon, I believe. We're going with Elaine, the woman I met at the Jubilee Jungle. I recently discovered that her birth name is Ariel. Her adoptive parents changed her name to Elaine. She agrees that we should call her Ariel to prevent confusion between the two of you."

"The name Ariel is an Old Testament name for Jerusalem," Elaine informed me.

"That's where she was born." Putting some bread into my carry bag, I added, "She's the daughter of a Jewess."

With that piece of news, Elaine jumped up and down like a child. "We're going to Jerusalem with a native Jew!"

I briefed her on our plans, not sure if she was listening. "We have to meet Ariel at the place of entry. *It really should be called something else now,* I thought. *Since we don't just come anymore but come and go.*

Putting salve and other items into my bag, I looked up to see Elaine walking down the flower-lined path in a daze. "Wait for me!" I ran to catch up with her.

We exchanged warm embraces with Ariel and had a brief catching-up and getting-acquainted time. Then, holding hands and closing our eyes, we waited to be transported.

I opened my eyes at the last second, hoping to see what happens when we travel through the heavens. Quicker than the speed of light, we arrived on earth. It didn't matter whether my eyes were open or closed.

"When the workload decreases, you may travel to earth by way of the stars and see the beauty of My creation," the Father spoke to my heart.

"Thank You, Father."

Scanning our surroundings, I saw that we had materialized on a hill overlooking the City of Jerusalem. A brilliant glare from the sun reflected off the golden pinnacle of the newly rebuilt temple.

The Holy City's beauty captivated us. It wasn't as glorious as the City of Our God in heaven, but there was so much rich history in Jerusalem: David reigned as king within her walls; Jesus died outside her wall; the church was birthed within her. Scripture flooded our hearts as we examined every detail.

"Jesus reigns here!" I said with a lump in my throat. We drank in the city's magnificence with tears in our eyes.

"Do you see the Sacred River flowing out of the city?" Ariel pointed to the east side of the city wall. The land along the river was lush green. People were harvesting leaves for medicine from the young fruit trees lining the riverbanks. Baskets of fruit waited on racks to be shipped.

What a beautiful sight! I thought. Much of earth's vegetation, including many of its trees, had burned or dried up during the tribulation period. New life now sprang up from the ground.

Pointing to men tilling the ground by irrigation ditches near the Sacred River, I said, "Look, it's time to sow."

"Let's go into the city, "Elaine suggested, obviously thrilled by the idea.

As we walked toward Jerusalem, our white robes changed into Israeli national garb. Elaine wore a jade-green veil draped over a loose-fitting light-green tunic. Ariel wore a long multicolored dress with a lavender veil that complemented her dark skin. My veil was blue and my tunic light-gray.

I was so busy taking in the character of the city as we walked that I didn't notice an elderly woman approaching with a basket. We collided. I knocked the basket out of her hands and seeds spewed into the air.

"I am so sorry," I bent to pick some up.

"It's okay." She started to help.

Elaine and Ariel helped us get most of the seeds back into the basket.

I continued with my apology: "I should have been paying more attention to where I was going."

"No, I was in too much of a hurry. It's time to sow, you know. After years of hunger, finally, there will be plenty. Plus, the true Bread of Heaven reigns in Jerusalem." Her face radiated with joy. "I'm Rachel Bathphilleo," she said, extending her hand.

I greeted her and was about to introduce Elaine and Ariel when I saw that Ariel's face had turned white. She was holding Rachel's basket and it was slipping from her fingers as she stood with her eyes fixed on Rachel. I took the basket to keep it from falling again.

Ariel spoke falteringly, "I'm Ariel Bathphilleo."

While searching Ariel's face, Rachel began to visibly shake. She asked Ariel where and when she had been born.

"Zion Hospital, Jerusalem, January 17."

I began to see a resemblance.

Rachel's eyes filled with tears. "My baby! . . . my baby! I can't believe it!" Her arms opened wide. Ariel moved toward her. They wept in each other's embrace. Elaine and I watched the precious reunion, crying too.

Eventually, Rachel held Ariel back from her so she could have a good look at her. "You were only a baby when I last saw you. How beautiful you are!"

Ariel blushed at her mother's praise. "I love you, Mother," she whispered.

Rachel's face etched in sorrow and she bowed her head. "How could you ever forgive me for giving you away? Timidly looking up again, she said. "When I left Israel, I didn't know how I could feed you."

"Mother,"— Ariel took her hand—"I forgave you long ago."

Rachel stared at her. "Well I can't forgive myself," she stammered, pulling her hand away.

"Please Mother, let's go into Jerusalem. We can have lunch and get to know each other."

"I can't enter the city. See those guards at the gates."

I recalled the Scripture verse that says no unclean person may enter the city. Rachel couldn't enter because her heart was full of unforgiveness.

"My sin is too great!" she sobbed.

"Father," I prayed, "She needs grace."

"He's here," the Father answered.

Jesus stood before us. Elaine covered her mouth with her hand, but a cry of joy still escaped. Ariel squealed "Jesus" and ran to hug Him. Rachel fell to her knees and covered her face.

After hugging Ariel, Jesus walked over to Rachel. He gently brought her back to her feet.

"Rachel, look at Me." He put His hand under her chin and lifted her face. "Look at Me." Tears flowed profusely down her cheeks. "Come into the city and dine with Me and your sisters."

She lowered her head again and turned it from side to side. "I'm not worthy to enter."

Jesus lifted her chin again. "Look at me, Rachel.

She lifted her eyes to His.

"When I gave My life on the cross, I defeated Satan and the powers of darkness. My blood cleansed the sins of all who believe in Me and obey Me. Do you believe that, Rachel?"

"Yes."

"Rachel, My blood removed *all* your sins."

Jesus' eyes were filled with such deep love that Rachel's heart melted. "I believe You, Jesus." Her body relaxed as if a great load had fallen off of her back. She smiled and made our joy complete.

"Let's go into the city," Jesus said with a smile. He extended His arms to Rachel and Ariel. Elaine and I joined hands and jubilantly followed them.

I thought again of the fallow ground outside the city.

"There is a time to sow," I said to Elaine. Watching Rachel lean on Jesus' arm, I added, "How precious are the seeds of forgiveness and the bloom of righteousness they produce."

Reminiscent of Zechariah's prophesy concerning ten men of different languages and nations taking hold of one Jew by the hem of his robe and saying, "Let us go with you. We've heard that God is with you," Elaine held on to the hem of Ariel's veil as we entered the city gates.

Chapter 34 -- Cave People

This was our fourth day preparing for the upcoming Coronation Celebration in Jerusalem. It would bring people from every nation of the world.

My husband and sons helped with makeshift housing in the surrounding pasturelands. The peripheral areas were already dotted with tents. Elaine, Ariel and I busied ourselves in the gymnasium of an elementary school that temporarily served as a workshop.

Bent over a sewing machine, I wondered how all the visitors would be fed. I had seen storehouses filled with fruits and vegetables, and I knew the wheat fields would ripen soon, so there would be plenty of bread and produce.

Then a thought struck me and I rapped my head impulsively. *Of course, Jesus would have no problem feeding a multitude! He multiplied loaves and fishes and He fed the Israelites with manna for forty years.* I had to smile at my shortsightedness.

I was helping Elaine and Ariel with a banner for the opening procession when the smell of burning meat flooded my nostrils. Looking through a doorway I saw smoke filling the sky above the temple.

Animal sacrifices had been renewed in remembrance of Jesus' sacrifice on Calvary. The animals' blood represented His completed work of salvation and their burning flesh symbolized our total surrender to Him as King.

"Father, all that You do is perfect," I said. "Thank You for allowing me to be a part of it." The Holy Spirit touched my heart and I rejoiced in His love.

As the sun began to set, I took a moment to rest. Instantly, I found myself on a mountain looking down over a valley. "Oh Father, it's so beautiful!" I could see a large body of water in the distance.

"That was once the Dead Sea," the Father told me. "Sacred water now flows to it from the temple in Jerusalem."

The sea was brimming with life; fishermen were again applying their trade. I wondered if Andrew was fishing out there.

"I guess they'll have to give it a new name," I said looking up.

"How about Resurrection Sea?" someone responded unexpectedly. I looked to my side to see none other than David, son of Jesse, smiling at me as he completed his upward climb. "It seems we're always ending up on the same mountain."

I was humbled by his presence. "It's so good to see you again, King David."

"There is only one King, my sister, and that is Jesus."

He stood beside me and looked out over the Dead Sea. "The Father sent me here to talk to you."

I stared at him in bewilderment.

"I've been perplexed over a particular situation." Looking back at me, he said, "The Father told me you have the solution to my dilemma."

"I have the solution?"

"Apparently so." He smiled while looking over some distant mountains. Pointing, he said, "We have some Christians holing up in a cave over there. We've tried everything to get them to come out, but they went through such horrors during the Time of Jacob's Trouble that they trust no one. Even if Jesus Himself would appear to them they would fear He was a false Messiah, a trick of the evil one. They know nothing of the great battle or of Jesus' reign as King." He paused before looking straight into my eyes and asking, "So how do we reach them?"

My mind went blank. *How indeed! Father, what is the answer?* I prayed earnestly in my heart.

An anointing of the Holy Spirit came over me bringing the answer.

"I have a bird friend, Camelia," I told King David. "You've met her."

He nodded.

"I also know a donkey named Martha. Together, they can do the job."

David's eyes brightened as if the Father were showing him the whole picture. "I remember Martha from the Palm Sunday procession," he said with a smile. "And I believe I've heard Jesus mention Martha and Camelia in one of His stories." He laughed wholeheartedly. "Yes, they can do the job! Thank you, dear sister."

With no further ado, Israel's prince turned and started down the mountain.

Alone again, I asked the Father, "Why didn't you just tell David the answer rather than have him ask me?"

"My children need to often be reminded that they are a part of a body. My help will often come to you through others. In that way, you will not be tempted to be self-sufficient and grow cold in your love for others."

"Father, You are so wise. I love You."

"I love you, My daughter. Now rest, for you and your dad must accompany Camelia and Martha to the cave."

I sat down by a tree and closed my eyes, but sleep was long in coming.

Chapter 35 -- The Donkey's Adventure

"Don't lean so far over the edge," Dad warned Martha for the third time. "You could fall." He walked on without waiting for us.

Martha couldn't resist smelling the plants on the edge of the mountain path. "So what if I fall," she muttered to me. "It's not like I'm going to hurt myself."

Martha was experiencing her first mission to earth. I felt sure Camelia was hoping it was also her last. She'd flown far ahead to get away from the friction between Dad and Martha.

Though Martha walked a little behind, I kept my ear tuned to her rhythmic hoofbeats. They had just stopped abruptly. I looked back to see her looking at me with a distraught expression.

"A thought just occurred to me," she confided. "If I did fall, I'd be the laughing stock of heaven. What would all my donkey friends think of me?" She shook her head fiercely, as though trying to shake the thought out. Then she lowered her head for a moment. She looked back at me and said, "Another thought just occurred to me. "It's that ugly pride lifting its head again, isn't it?" With an upward thrust of her hind legs, she pretended to give the old pride a sendoff. "That'll fix you!" she snorted, then brayed a loud laugh.

Dad heard her and turned to scowl at her. "You and I are going to have a little talk when we get back." He frowned at her until she lowered her head again. Satisfied that she was repentant, he turned and started up the mountain once more.

Martha waited until he was far enough ahead that he couldn't hear her before confiding in me again: "I like his little talks. He never says much, just lays out the facts plain and simple." I smiled, identifying with her. She went on: "A lot of his thinking, though, is still so earthbound. I find it very interesting."

It had always seemed to me that my dad had unlimited patience. *Could it be that Martha is in his life to help him grow in patience?* I recalled how Moses was still able to grow in humility. *I guess it's possible!*

"Martha," I said, "I don't think you should try to get Dad upset. That's wrong, you know."

It was easy to see that the idea was a new concept for her. A breeze of the Holy Spirit swept around her head and she soon appeared enlightened.

"I never thought of it that way before." She sighed. "I'm going to miss those little talks." Lowering her head, she started walking faster up the mountain.

Camelia landed on my shoulder. "I think things will be better now," I said.

Camelia chirped "Yes" as though she already knew. I should have guessed she would have talked to the Father about it.

We finally reached the mouth of the cave. With a serious look, Dad told Camelia and Martha they had to go in without him. He checked Martha's saddle bag to be sure it had all the necessary supplies, including a bottle of sacred water and a pouch of healing leaves from the young trees along the Sacred River. "If you need help, come and get us," he told them.

Camelia looked at Dad while bending her head to the

right and left. Martha said, nonchalantly, "Well Birdie, if you're coming with me, we'd better get going."

Camelia chirped wildly and flew in circles around Martha's head.

Martha bellowed, "Birdie, you're making me dizzy!"

Camelia lighted on my shoulder, her little chest puffed out.

"Martha, Camelia hates to be called Birdie," I said firmly.

Martha curled her lips up in a smile. "Oh, I see. Sorry about that, Camelia." Camelia's body relaxed a little. "If your feathers are smoothed down now, let's go."

When Martha said go, I thought Camelia might have been transported. She disappeared, into the cave, I guess.

Martha smiled and said, "I had my doubts when the Father told me I was going on this mission with a bird, but she's actually very spunky." She kept talking as she ambled into the cave: "Never would have thought it . . . . Just goes to show you never can tell what someone might be like . . . she's ok . . . didn't understand . . . ."

When she was far enough into the cave that we couldn't hear her, Dad and I looked at each other and we could each tell that the other was deciding to spend some time in prayer.

"Think it'll take a miracle," Dad sighed.

We made ourselves comfortable under the shade of a wild olive tree. After we each had spoken to the Father, Dad filled me in on the latest news of our family members still living on earth. The Father had scheduled a one-day layover in Wisconsin for him before he'd arrived in Jerusalem. He'd stayed with my brother Victor. My sisters Donna and Marian had been able to spend the day with them. And my youngest sister Lori had managed to see him for a short time just before he came to Jerusalem.

After telling me all the news, he got up and walked to a point where there was a panoramic view of the valley below. Nodding in the direction of Jerusalem, he said, "The fields are turning green."

I walked over and could see the fields' green hues. They looked like the fields I had watched being seeded earlier in my mission.

In the other direction, toward the north, several military tanks and vehicles remained in a battle-scarred field. We were content to not mention them. When Dad noticed me surveying them, he said, "Well, we might have a long wait here. I suppose we could go sit down."

We waited at the mouth of the cave for a long time. I was beginning to wonder if we should go in and get Martha and Camelia.

"They're fine," the Father told me. "Be patient like your dad." I looked over at Dad. He was sleeping braced up against a tree.

"Father, I give You my impatience. Please give me Your patience, and Your peace." I felt His peace fill my spirit. "Father, how long will it be before I rid myself of my old earthly thinking?"

"You have overcome, Daughter. As for how long your old ways may yet trouble you, does it really matter?"

Becoming aware of my impatience again, I had to laugh. My laughter woke up Dad.

"Is Martha back?" he asked, assuming I was laughing at her.

"No, Dad, I was just laughing at my impatience. Wait, I do hear someone in the cave."

"Camelia, you're all right," Martha was saying.

Camelia chirped, "Just watch where you're walking."

We could hear other voices too. Martha exited the cave with Camelia on her head and two small children on her back. Five men and two women, all appearing Middle Eastern, walked alongside them. Their skin seemed unusually light. I imagined it was due to their long stay in the dark cave. They appeared to have otherwise weathered their ordeal rather well. I assumed that was due to the provisions for healing we had sent in with Martha.

Dad attempted to speak to them in their language and

before long he was conversing with them. He had studied many Arabic dialects in heaven in preparation for missions like this.

Though not able to understand their words, I couldn't mistake their excitement and great relief. I smiled warmly at the children and was blessed by bright, loving smiles in return. Dad introduced me to the men and women; they all spoke to me at once with smiling faces. I nodded and returned their smiles.

As we followed an old path down the mountainside, I was curious about what Martha and Camelia had done to get them to come out of the cave. "How did you do it, Camelia?" I asked when she lighted on my shoulder

She told me the whole story. In short, the cave people knew that Martha had been sent by God because no human or demon could come up with someone like Martha. Her chirping revealed how proud she was of Martha.

Whatever else may have happened in that cave, I could see that Martha and Camelia had become good friends, and that was most certainly a miracle.

"Martha's first mission to earth turned out to be quite an adventure," I said. Camelia kissed my cheek and then flew back to ride on Martha's head.

Chapter 36 -- Return to the Valentine Garden

It was great to be back in my heavenly home. I had spent so much time on earth over the past few months that I had gotten homesick. I sat on the window seat in my drawing room appreciating items that enhanced the room's beauty. From the drawing room I could see the family room, dining area and library. I was enthralled with all that I saw.

It wasn't that my spirit was covetous; rather, I entertained a deep joy and gratefulness for God's beauty and holiness that soaked every item. I praised and thanked the Father for each piece of furniture, each window, each doorway. My home was a visible expression of God's heart as I knew Him.

The coronation would be in a few days and then my earthly duties would begin to diminish. All that aside for the moment, I communed with the Father.

Closing my eyes, I became aware of chirping outside the window near the golden tree. Alice was telling Camelia she was glad to have her home again. Camelia was clearly enjoying her nest and Alice's company.

Releasing a sigh of contentment, an earthly song about coming home to heaven came to my mind:

I'm going home where the streets are made of gold
And the walls of precious stone,
Where the river of life flows freely from the Throne
And the trees bear their fruit in each season.

Heaven was this and so much more! How surprised the people I knew on earth would be when they actually saw it. Picturing their faces made me laugh. This was home as they had never experienced home before, not even in the best of homes.

A breeze of the Holy Spirit blew through the window fanning my hair. I laughed again with pure pleasure at the tingling sensation of His kiss.

While delighting in my home and the Holy Spirit's sweet communion, I noticed my husband walking up the path to my door. He'd just returned from an earthly mission. I greeted him at the door with a big smile and hug, both of which he lovingly returned. He sat with me on my window seat and we silently enjoyed each other's presence. We were not the married couple we had been on earth, but brother and sister in the Lord.

He said, "What do you say we visit the Valentine Garden? You've told me so much about it, but I've still never seen it."

"Let's ask the Father."

Before we asked, a breeze of the Spirit floated us through the large window into the sky. We held hands looking down at the rich, lustrous beauty of heaven. "Even Jerusalem can't hold a candle to this," he commented.

When we floated over the Golden Sea, I pointed to the whale playing out in the deep. "I rode that whale."

A little later we could see the Jubilee Jungle off to our right. Bunkeys played in the trees while lions slept in a grassy meadow.

My husband shook his head at the lions. "It seems like all they do is sleep."

I laughed. "I guess that's heaven to them."

Soon we saw the bright red glow of the Valentine Garden. The Spirit gently set us down on the flower-laden grass.

"Would you look at that!" he said. "Even the grass has little valentine hearts." He bent to pick one. After looking it over carefully, he handed it to me. It reminded me of the special flower Jesus had given me. With my heart filled with rapturous love, I kissed it and the little flower flew into the sky.

"Where's it going?" my husband asked.

"To Jesus," I told him blissfully.

He held my hand as we walked through the garden. When we came upon a massive tree loaded with hearts, he squinted to look it over. "It's so bright! I should have brought my sunglasses."

"You don't have sunglasses," I reminded him laughingly.

He walked over to the tree for a closer look and reached as high as he could on his tiptoes to pick a large heart, bright red, with a small white heart at its center. He gave it to me saying, "This is you, my valentine. The Lord made your heart clean and pure like this little white heart."

I took the valentine and hugged him. It was my turn to search the tree for a fitting valentine. I spotted a large red cushion-soft heart. I picked it and handed it to him. "To my valentine, whose heart the Lord has made soft and gentle. I love you." He smiled in the manner of a small boy and kissed my cheek.

Holding our treasured valentines, we walked over a bridge and up a hill near the garden's edge. Sitting under a sycamore tree we gazed out over the garden.

Our love was different in heaven. It wasn't sensual or indulgent, or even romantic, though we hugged often. It was a feeling of completeness, an intertwining and melting of our spirits and souls with God's—an ecstasy unlike any on earth. I suppose a few husbands and wives might have momentarily attained a limited measure of this sort of experience while on earth, but here the feeling was not fleeting—it never waned cold or grew old.

The love my husband and I experienced was one of our richest blessings. *God is love*, I thought. Our hearts were so full of God's love that we simultaneously broke into praise to the Father.

"Thank You, Father, for my wife, my friend, my sister in the Lord."

"Thank You, Father, for my husband, my friend, my brother in the Lord, the man you gave me to love."

A breeze of the Spirit floated us back into the sky. Looking down at the shrinking garden, I felt that the Father had deepened our love.

Chapter 37 – The Coronation

Dressed in my celebration robe with flowers braided into the tresses of my hair, I looked around at my children and thought, *These are the finishing touches to the beauty God has given me.* While marveling at their glorious smiling faces, I paraphrased Scripture to them: "Your children shall be as jewels strung around your neck." They did indeed shine like brilliant jewels, though actually more like the sparkling stars that the prophet Daniel described in Scripture, due to their shimmering white robes.

My husband nodded and reached for my hand. Joined in a circle at the place of entry, we all descended to the sky above Jerusalem.

"This is the first time everyone in heaven will gather with those on earth for worship," I commented to my husband. He looked at me as if he'd been thinking the same thought.

The gathering crowd of saints reminded me of the story of Christ's birth: how the sky above Bethlehem's pasturelands had filled with hosts of angels praising and glorifying God. How breathtaking it was to be a part of this heavenly crowd saturating the sky above the Holy City.

"Every angel, brother, sister, and creature of heaven is here to witness Jesus' coronation," Clint commented. "It's profoundly awesome!" Camelia and Alice, both perched on his shoulder, chirped in agreement. They had gold ribbons decorated with shiny silver bows around their necks.

"They're so darling," Elaine whispered to me.

Cute though they were, Camelia still didn't like being fussed over, so I responded silently with a smile.

Mother and Dad joined our group. Dad led Martha who wore a lavish flower wreath around her neck that Mother had made for her. Martha was so busy staring at people on earth that she didn't notice us.

When she finally looked up, our friend Ariel had joined us, sporting a bunkey on her shoulder. Martha and the bunkey made eye contact. Each gave the other a serious look.

Unexpectedly, the bunkey's top lip drew up in a wide grin. Martha answered with a soft bray. I breathed a sigh of relief.

I watched the bunkey for a moment wondering how it would behave. The little fellow was too overwhelmed for any hysterical laughter.

By this time, most of our relatives had joined our group. Travis commented, "The sky is so filled with citizens of heaven that we're blocking the sun for the people on earth." He laughed at the thought.

The light on earth did indeed look different. *It looks more like the light in heaven,* I thought. *The glory of God must be reflecting off of us onto earth to give it that golden tone.*

We had all been excited about Jesus' coronation since His return to heaven after the great battle. Now we were experiencing a fresh anointing of the Holy Spirit. Tears flowed down our faces to our robes, making them mirror even more of heaven's luster.

The angels began a song of praise and the citizens of heaven joined in the chorus. On the second stanza, the choirs of earth joined in. A wonderful feeling of unity and oneness enveloped us as we worshiped Jesus together:

Thou art worthy, Thou art worthy, Thou art worthy, O Lord
To receive honor, glory and power;
For Thou hast created all things.
And for Thy pleasure they are created.

David pulled on my sleeve and pointed to earth. Processions of kings carrying gifts were approaching the throne. It looked as though all nations were represented among the offering bearers. He cited Scripture: " 'The kings of Tarshish and of the islands will bring presents, the kings of Sheba and Seba offer gifts.' "

The spectacle on earth was glorious! With all the different nationalities present in clusters, most wearing their national dress, they looked like a multicolored quilt. I could only imagine how we looked to them. The Book of Revelation described us as a crystal sea of glass.

Trumpets joyously heralded, interrupting our singing. They sounded a second time. Then a silence filled with anticipation covered the heavens and the earth. We looked to the east, the direction from which Jesus would come. A bright star moved toward us. Jesus was coming!

As He drew nearer, light from His presence passed through pockets of moisture creating a rainbow of colors. As He drew nearer still, we fell to our knees and bowed our heads. I looked up as He passed. His glory was blinding—far brighter than the sun! He passed through the heavenly crowd on His descent to His throne.

When the people on earth saw Him passing through the multitudes of heaven they fell to the ground, face down. More trumpet calls filled the air when He reached His throne. His face gloriously shone with love as He looked back up into the heavens at us and then around Him at the people of earth.

With a sob caught in my throat, I continued to watch. The light around Jesus softened to a golden glow. The Father shielded the people on earth from the powerful anointing so they could kneel to watch the coronation. They rose to their knees staring in wonder at Jesus.

This was the first time for many people of earth to see Him in His glorified form. He wore a pure white robe that reached to His feet and a golden sash tied around His chest. His head and hair were white as snow. His eyes burned like fiery coals and His feet were like fired bronze.

While the citizens of earth gazed at Him, the hands of the Father appeared in the sky above His head, drawing cries and gasps of surprise. A golden crown covered with jewels materialized in His hands. The Holy Spirit descended from heaven as a dove and lighted on Jesus' shoulder.

The voice of the Father thundered throughout the heavens: "This is My Son! In Him, I am well pleased. He is your King!" The father's hands placed the crown on Jesus' head. It gave a display of sparks like fireworks when it touched His hair.

Trumpets again pierced the air, but this time with the accompaniment of musical instruments. The angels burst into praises: "Hallelujah! Praise to the King! Praise to the Lamb of God!"

Then, once again, there was a holy silence. The hands of the Father drew back from the crown and opened outward, palms down, as if giving a blessing. Then they vanished and the Holy Spirit dove flew back to heaven.

All eyes rested on Jesus. Having changed back into His human form, He held His arms out wide in a gesture of receiving the people of earth. The multitudes broke into jubilant songs of worship and praise. Jesus stepped back to sit on His throne.

While the people of earth celebrated their new King, we floated back to heaven. There, we would continue our celebration with the Father and the Holy Spirit. Camelia and Alice were already dancing and singing on Clint's shoulder. Everyone hugged and kissed.

When Jesus would return to heaven, He would meet us in His human form and we would all affectionately congratulate Him. I could hardly wait. *Even in this I must learn patience*, I thought.

A worship dance began and I joined the dancers, praising the Father with uplifted hands.

Chapter 38 -- The Bunkeys' Match

Not long after Jesus' coronation, I gazed over the green valley and distant mountains visible from where I rested by the Sacred River. I bit into a perfect yellow apple from a bowl of fruit resting on my lap.

"Can I have a bite?" someone asked in a gruff voice. To my surprise, Arman peeked over my shoulder desirously eying my apples.

"Of course you can, Arman." I put an apple in his mouth and watched him devour it with one bite. He then trotted over to the bank and got a drink from the sacred water. When he finished drinking, he lifted his head and back and whinnied, pawing the air with his front hooves.

"It's been a long time since I've seen you, Arman. What have you been doing?"

He whinnied laughingly and said, "I just came from an interesting mission on earth." He snorted another laugh.

"Oh, please tell me about it."

He loped back to where I sat, bent his hind knees and sat down on the grass next to me.

"The Father told me about a gorilla in a Congo jungle in Africa that was terrorizing some village people near Owando. You're aware, I'm sure, that earth's wild animals have made peace with humans."

"Yes."

"But not Jumbo! No angel or human could get near Jumbo. The huge gorilla had found a tree house in what he considered to be his jungle and had taken it over—causing its inhabitants to flee for their lives. So, the Father had developed a plan: I and some of my friends were to carry bunkeys down to earth who would teach old Jumbo a new way of life."

My interest heightened when he mentioned the bunkeys.

I imagined the horses of fire flying to earth with bunkeys laughing hysterically and rolling on their backs.

"How did you handle their hysterical laughter and their rolling on your backs?"

Arman looked at me as though he could not believe my question. "They didn't dare laugh or roll on our backs; we were on a mission."

"I see," I said, though I didn't completely understand. I remembered the bunkey who had acted normal at the coronation and thought, *Maybe I've misjudged them.*

Arman continued: "When we reached the jungle, the bunkeys went to find Jumbo. Not wanting to miss anything, my friends and I followed above the trees so we could watch.

"When they found Jumbo's hut, they made their presence known to the king gorilla. Jumbo looked down at them and snorted. He beat his chest in a show of power. So the bunkeys beat their chests. That made Jumbo furious—and he was not alone. He and his fellow gorillas descended from the hut and formed a circle around the bunkeys. Jumbo beat his chest again and grunted loudly in a hoot-like series. The bunkeys grunted as loudly as they could while vigorously beating their chests. Then they laughed and rolled on the ground.

Ah, I thought, *that I'm familiar with.*

"At that, Jumbo picked up a bunkey and threw him against a tree. The bunkey got up, laughed and rolled on the ground again. That looked like fun to the rest of the bunkeys, so they all ran to Jumbo for their turn. The rougher Jumbo treated them the harder the bunkeys laughed and the faster they came back for more.

"The other gorillas backed off and looked on in shock. The enraged Jumbo, being unable to comprehend what was happening, became more and more frustrated and bewildered. He finally grew so fatigued that he sat down and hung his head in defeat. The bunkeys came and sat on his lap and hugged him, pulling on his ears lovingly.

"Then Ariel, our friend from the Jubilee Jungle, arrived with some people from a nearby village. The people were afraid of the gorillas at first, but when they saw how timid Jumbo was with the bunkeys they came nearer. Ariel handed Jumbo a banana, which he took eagerly. After that, the villagers were able to feed him. And now they have no more trouble from Jumbo."

"I guess I never thought that the animals of earth would need to be retrained," I said. "What a marvelous mission!"

Arman gave me a wide smile before pulling his hind legs under him to get up on all four again. "Time to get back to the stables. By the way, I have some friends who would love some of those delicious apples." He looked longingly at the fruit in my bowl.

"Take them. I'll pick more." Realizing that he wouldn't be able to carry them, I looked up, "Father, I need a way for Arman to carry the apples." A gust of wind brought a brown bag to my feet. "Thank You, Father." I put the apples in the bag and put its twine handle between Arman's teeth. He nodded thanks and then bolted into the sky.

As I watched him go, I was thankful to have heard his story about Jumbo and the bunkeys. The bunkeys' ability to love Jumbo even though he mistreated them gave me a new respect for the little creatures.

Only God's love could do that, I thought. It made me wonder: *If Christ's followers on earth were more willing to give God their wounds and rejections and allow His love to control their lives, how many human "Jumbos" would be changed?*

The Father spoke to my heart: "The person who empties his or her heart of all that is not of Me, and thus allows My love to flow to another, will be blessed and changed even if the other person rejects My love."

"Oh Father, Your ways are so perfect! Thank You for Your perfect love."

Chapter 39 – A Sister's Dream

Lois and I sat at her dining table looking out the window at Trinity Lake, one of heaven's many fishing lakes. My sister and her husband Bill had arrived in heaven at the time of the ingathering. Having obtained a special dispensation from the Father to share a home in heaven, they lived together here on the shore of Trinity.

Mother and Dad often sailed over from Dad's rustic home on the other side of the lake to visit them. The four spent peaceful times fishing. They never ate the fish they caught; they just reveled in the fun of catching them. And the fish enjoyed their flights through the air chomping down on hook-free bait.

We had been talking, but at the moment she was staring out the window at the lake with a distracted look about her.

"I had a bizarre dream," she confessed.

"I've never heard of anyone dreaming in heaven."

"I never have either," she agreed. "But I had a dream—a frightening dream!"

I was shocked. "What was it about?"

"I, I, I"—she stuttered uncharacteristically—"dreamed I was fishing out on the lake"—she looked out the window again—"when a large fish came out of the water and swallowed me and my boat."

My first impulse was to laugh, but seeing the startled look on her face I suppressed it. "What do you think it means?"

"Let me tell you the whole story." She nervously took a long drink and then began.

I'm sitting in this boat inside this large fish, and I'm thinking, *This is just like Jonah in the whale, except Jonah wasn't in a boat.* I tried to remember what he had done to get out. *He prayed to the Lord*, I recalled. *But what did he pray? And why was he in the whale in the first place?* I started to panic.

I heard splashing. Someone was walking through the water. Then I heard a match being struck and alarmingly saw the face of an old man. He looked like the character portrayed in the novel *The Old Man and the Sea.*

"May I sit with you?" he asked with a smile. "I'm Jonah." He crawled into the boat.

My heart started beating more normally again. "You're the Jonah in the Bible?"

"The one and only." He gave a sailor's salute. "And you are Lois." He held up the burning match so he could search my face.

I wondered how he knew my name, but I was more concerned about getting out of the whale. "How did you get out of the whale?"

"Oh yes, the whale." He looked around before saying, "Perhaps a better question would be 'How did I get into the whale?'"

I told him I knew how he had gotten into the whale.

"Yes," he said, "but you don't know what I was thinking. When the sailors threw me overboard, I thought I was ready to die rather than preach to the Ninevites. It took sinking to the bottom of the sea and having seaweed wrap around my head to make me realize I was in no spiritual condition to meet my maker. My heart was full of unforgiveness and resentment. I repented and cried out to God and He caused a great whale to swallow me. It had air in its belly."

I noticed the match still burning. *There's air in this fish too*, I thought, *but it still should burn out.*

Jonah understood my thoughts and said, "This

is an eternal flame of truth."

Too frightened to think about that, my mind went back to his biblical story. "Why did you stay in the whale for three days?"

"That wasn't my plan." He frowned. "God knew that, even though I repented, I still needed to resolve to obey Him. I needed more time to forego my justifiable hate and righteous vengeance. It took three days of the whale's stomach acid eating at my flesh for me to submit to God's wisdom. He lowered his head. "I'm proud and stubborn."

"Well, it all turned out okay, right? You got out of the whale and you preached to the Ninevites."

"Yes, after the whale spit me out onto dry land, I preached to the Ninevites. But I wasn't happy when they repented. I still hadn't given God all of my pain and resentment."

He looked at me as though gazing right into my spirit and asked, "Would you hold this, please," handing the match to me. I took it wondering why he wanted me to hold it.

Then he disappeared and I woke up.

I waited for her to say more. She stared down the hallway toward her room. "I want to show you something."

I followed her to her room and, to my amazement, saw the match still burning inside a glass bowl!

"Have you talked to the Father about this?"

"It all happened shortly before you arrived. I will definitely ask Him." She stared again at the burning match.

"You know," I said, "sometimes we bury things so deep in our spirits that we don't even realize they're there." As I spoke, the flame flickered brighter and higher.

Just then a breeze of the Holy Spirit blew in from her garden terrace and whirled around her. The flame rose up and illuminated her face. Tears streamed down her cheeks.

Before long, I saw a gentle peace settle on her expressive features. We hugged and laughed in the Spirit. All fear was gone from her eyes and deep love shone from them.

The Father asked me to leave so He could speak with her.

"I'm terribly sorry to be abrupt," I said, "but I really must go."

I looked back before closing the door to discover that the match had disappeared. I sensed that the flame was now inside her. I was sure she and the Father would have a splendid talk. *Maybe Jonah will join them.*

Chapter 40 -- Ruler of a City

The classroom work completed, the real work was poised to begin. Jesus had assigned thousands of heaven's citizens as chief administrators of earth's cities and provinces. Most had been assigned to the region where they'd lived on earth. Some had been given a choice in the appointment.

My sons visited me with news of how each had been assigned a city to rule. David and Travis felt well trained and eager to start their overseeing posts. They delineated some of their plans to each other.

Clint's face, on the other hand, revealed a frightened little boy. I stroked his arm and said, "Let's go for a walk." He put his arm around me and we walked to the golden pathway by my home. We strolled in silence until we reached a lovely park with tall willows circling a small pond. The pond's crystal water was home to a beautiful snow goose, swimming grandly at its center.

Clint sat beside a willowy plant by the water and indicated that I should join him. I watched his furrowed brow while he gazed at the goose. After a while he looked at me intently and began to share his concerns.

"There have been monarchies in many parts the world. The Roman emperors once ruled most of the known world. But Jesus rules every nation! And His government is a theocracy!"

He picked a beautiful cream-colored bud in the shape of an open scroll from the plant and threw it out into the pond. That brought the snow goose over to inspect it.

"I think it's used to being fed," he said with a smile.

"Well, it won't starve to death anyway," I returned with a grin.

He gave me an indulgent smile, but quickly turned serious again. "There's so much to do in the city I'm to rule. The war took its toll on its buildings—what was left of them after the earthquakes. Crime has been so prevalent that it won't be easy enforcing Jesus' laws. Jesus must rule with a rod of iron you know, and administer justice quickly and severely." He watched to see what my reaction would be.

I shrugged and said, "That's the way it has to be."

He nodded. "There's a great need for employment. And the education system must be converted to a Christ-centered curriculum. There's no end to the needs, Mother. I feel completely overwhelmed." He waited for my response.

"I understand. Please come with me. I want to take you somewhere."

He trustingly walked with me to a part of heaven that I'd heard much about but had never actually seen—the sector where the angels fellowship between their missions.

An angel in dazzling white tunic with glistening gold belt met us as soon as we stepped into the region. He wore luminous white trousers underneath his tunic and his sandals glistened of pure gold.

"The Father said you were coming." He smiled and pointed to a bench of gold so pure it reflected like glass. "Please have a seat. Sariano will be here soon." With no further words, he turned and continued down a path intersecting with ours.

As we sat down Clint asked, "Who is Sariano?"

"That would be I," said an angel appearing before us. He glowed iridescent blue, his tunic and his body. His eyes arrested ours. They blazed like burning coals. We feebly rose to our feet.

He extended his hand to Clint. "You must be Clint, the administrator of my city."

I could see that Clint was more than a little taken back.

"The Father assigned me to your city long before you were born," Sariano informed him.

Clint ventured a smile and replied, "I believe Jesus did say angels would be helping us." A glimmer came into his eyes as he inspected Sariano. The angel must have stood more than seven feet tall and weighed over four hundred pounds. From the muscles bulging under his tunic he was without a doubt a warrior angel.

"I feel a lot better now that I've met you," Clint said with relief showing all over his face.

Sariano's fire-like eyes peered into Clint's. "I see that you have been a little fearful about this assignment."

Clint looked down under his gaze. "I guess so. Most of my earthly life I lived to please others or myself, but now I want more than anything to please Jesus."

"And that you shall!" Sariano said triumphantly. The huge angel sat down and motioned for us to do the same. As soon as we sat down, several of his associates appeared before us. "Take a good look at these angels."

We obediently looked at the glorious beings. Sariano looked them over, as well, and said, "In spite of all the power you see here—" He looked at us and interrupted himself. "Allow me to use an earthly expression—I would be 'scared to death' to attempt a mission with all our power combined."

When we gaped in confusion, he provided an illustration: "Lucifer thought he could rule by his great power and might, and so did his followers. His followers were angels similar to these. Alas, we know where they are now."

"In a prison called the Abyss," I breathed.

The fire in Sariano's eyes dimmed. His voice quieted as he said, "Some of my friends were deceived by Lucifer." He soon regained his vigor and said, "Clint, you and I will not stumble as long as we allow Jesus to rule through us. We will never take our eyes off of our great King. Thus, we will please Him." He finished speaking with a fierce look of determination and an arm raised victoriously.

In the next moment he looked up and seemed to listen to instructions. He looked back at us and said, "The Father says I must leave now for a mission." He shook Clint's hand, saying, "We will fellowship often." He then gave me a wide, loving smile.

"Thank you, Sariano," Clint said, his voice betraying his shaken emotions. "I'm ready now to do the work the Lord has given me."

Sariano was gone.

"Thank You Father," I prayed with my arm around my son.

Chapter 41 -- Camelia's Reprieve

Part of Camelia's ministry on earth was helping carnivorous birds change to herbivores. Most were willing, but there was one flock of vultures that refused, not listening to Camelia or other birds sent to help them.

"They're proud birds and they love the taste of blood," Camelia said, wings flapping. "Twice they tried to eat *me*! I just passed through their midst and sat on a branch watching them look for me."

"There's plenty of fruit and grain for them to eat now," I said. "I suppose you talked to the Father about it."

Camelia hopped impatiently on her little legs and tilted her head from side to side eyeing me.

"I guess that was a dumb question. Of course you've talked to the Father. What did He suggest?"

She ruffled her feathers and chirped, "He said I should put something on their meat that tastes bad. So I did. At first, they spat it out, but then they kept trying to eat it until they could, all the while leering at me defiantly."

Succumbing to her old bad habit, Camelia started flying circles around my head. Quickly, though, she caught herself and rested beside me.

"The Father says I can have a time of reprieve before I go back to work with them again," she said. "Come with me to the deep forest, pleeeeease."

I agreed to go and a breeze of the Holy Spirit picked us up and floated us toward the forest.

"I don't even have to flap my wings," she chirped happily with her little head lifted high so the breeze could fan out her feathers.

I had never been to the deep forest, a favorite place for birds and animals of heaven. I thought, *Heaven seems to have everything for everyone—everything good that is.* I looked down and noticed that the homes were quite different in this part of heaven. Built of stone and stucco with a Spanish flair, they were divinely beautiful.

We floated over the deep forest until the gentle breeze set us down through an opening in the trees. Standing in the midst of tall unusual plants, I peered into the dense growth.

"It's so dark! I'm surprised God's light doesn't penetrate more."

"The birds and animals like it this way," Camelia informed me offhandedly while flying to a nearby tree. "It was nice floating on the breeze, but I like flying better. It's fun to go fast." She demonstrated flying from tree to tree, trailed by a streak of white light.

"Camelia dear, you'll wear yourself out." I couldn't help but smile.

Without warning she said, "I'm going to visit some of my friends," and she was gone.

I looked around at the beautiful, densely foliaged trees decked with blue-green moss and ribbons of lacy, flowing vines.

"Oh, Father, Your creation is so beautiful!" I breathed in the fresh forest air, feeling the Father's presence. "Thank You for sharing all this with us. I love You so much." My heart was swollen with gratitude and love.

"All that I have is yours," the Father replied.

I sat down and leaned against a tree, then closed my eyes in blissful serenity. I must have slept because I awoke with a start. *What's all that noise?* My eyes opened to the marvelous sight of all the trees within view dressed with chirping, colorful birds of all sizes.

Camelia lighted on my shoulder and explained: "The Father said my friends could help me with the vultures."

"What do you plan to do?"

She lifted her head and said adamantly, "We won't allow them to eat anything but fruits and vegetables."

I could imagination the confrontation that would cause, and smiled. Camelia danced on my shoulder while the other birds chirped spiritedly. There was victory in the air.

Camelia then flew to my hand where she looked up at me and said, "We're leaving now."

I watched them fly into the air and disappear over the trees. A breeze of the Spirit picked me up and floated me out of the forest and back toward my home. From high above the trees I could see the cloud of birds beginning their descent to earth.

"Father, You're often forced to teach Your people in the same way You're about to teach those vultures. If only we would learn to consult You first, so You wouldn't have to take something away from us in order to get us to listen to You. I know I've been like those vultures many times."

The Father touched me with His encouraging love in the same way one would put his arms around a small child to say I love you.

Chapter 42 -- What's the Matter with Rita?

On one particularly memorable mission during this time Elaine and I ministered to a young Chinese couple in the city where our younger sister Rita ministered. We eagerly made arrangements to meet Rita in a small park near the church her singles group attended.

Sitting beneath a blooming magnolia tree, Elaine and I listened while Rita extolled her group. It was a small group compared to others in the city. Nonetheless, Rita was as enthusiastic about it as if it were an association of thousands. She enjoyed her leadership role with the singles so much that the Father had made it a permanent component of her mission work on earth.

In her usual buoyant manner, she told Elaine and me, "There are only twenty people in the group, but they're all so hungry for the things of God that I love my work with them. They cleaned up the whole city. The streets and parks sparkle, pollution-free. They picked up thousands of beer cans and cigarette wrappers, and mountains of fast-food wrappers. Doesn't the park look and smell fresh and clean?" She beamed with pleasure while taking a deep breath.

"America the beautiful," I sang while surveying the park. She and Elaine laughed.

"What is your group doing now that the cleanup is finished?" Elaine asked.

"They can't help people enough. There's not a widow or orphan in the city that hasn't been blessed by them."

Elaine and I listened attentively to stories of people whom the group had helped. Rita had a special gift for transmitting the joy of the Lord and it was overflowing in our hearts.

"Praise You, Father!" Elaine said raising her hands toward heaven.

"Have you noticed how different people are now?" Rita said. "They're not like they were when we lived on earth."

"Under Jesus' rule, it's a vastly different world," I reminded her.

"I realize that. But still, the tremendous spiritual growth I see here is amazing." Her face glowed. "There's a young man in my singles group that is such a dynamic Christian. His name is Thomas. He's the epitome of Christianity— always complimentary, always eager to please, totally on fire for God! I've asked him to give the teaching at our meeting tonight. You really should come and hear him." She almost literally bounced with enthusiasm.

Her praise of Thomas was cut short by the shouts of children playing ball on the diamond in the park. The batter had hit the ball toward the lawn where we sat and a little fielder was running backward toward us trying to catch the fly. He tripped over a small stone marker and hit his head on a monument. Everyone ran to him.

His small body lay motionless with his eyes slightly opened. Elaine knelt beside him and listened for his breathing. She then searched for a pulse in the hollow of his neck.

"Is he hurt?" a little girl asked, not able to see the boy through the crowd.

An older boy standing next to me, acting as though he were making a pronouncement, said, "He's dead." Elaine searched the boy's wrist for a pulse then looked up at Rita and me nodding sadly.

In complete composure, Rita told the children, "We're going to pray for him." Elaine and I laid our hands on the boy along with her while she prayed aloud: "Father, we ask that Your healing power enter into this boy. We ask in the name of Your Son, Jesus."

Having brought our petition to the Father, with closed eyes we offered prayers of praise and thanksgiving.

"It didn't work," a young girl said. "God didn't hear your prayers."

"God always hears our prayers when our hearts are upright before Him," Rita responded gently. "He doesn't always answer in the way we think is best, but He always answers."

Tears started falling from the young girl's eyes. The children stood white-faced and red-eyed looking down at their playmate.

Suddenly, the boy gasped for air. Then he sneezed loudly. Finally, he opened his eyes.

"He's alive!" the children squealed jumping up and down.

Elaine and I helped him to his feet. The doubting young girl was the first to give him a big hug.

"Cut it out, Christy!" he objected.

Everyone laughed in great relief.

When the children started back to play ball, I could see

that the young boy was a little wobbly on his feet, so I asked him to stay and sit by us for a while. Checking the bump on his head, I found it to be no more than a minor injury now. I introduced myself and my sisters to him.

"What's your name?" Elaine asked.

"Cory."

"You look just like a young man in my singles group," Rita said. "His name is Thomas Bilmore."

"That's my brother." He shrugged sheepishly.

Rita was effervescent again. "Oh! I'm so happy that your brother is in my group."

"He shouldn't be in that church group," the boy said matter-of-factly. Rubbing his head, he added, "He doesn't really follow Jesus."

Rita's face went blank. "What do you mean?"

Cory's small face expressed his displeasure. "He told me he wishes he could go back to the good old days when people were allowed to do what they pleased."

Tears started to fill Rita's eyes.

"Do you feel that way too?" Elaine asked Cory.

"Oh no!" he said. "I like things the way they are. I love Jesus!"

Tears now streamed from Rita's eyes. She left us, walking toward the church.

"What's the matter with Rita?" Cory asked, not understanding her sorrow.

With a heavy heart, I told him, "She needs to talk with the Father."

"Well, she'll be fine then," he said matter-of-factly again.

Elaine and I looked at each other. The Holy Spirit filled us with peace.

"Yes, she will," I said, smiling at Cory and giving him a big hug.

Cory squirmed away. "I'm going back to play ball." Running toward the diamond, he called back, "Thank you."

"You're welcome," Elaine and I yelled after him.

Rita returned from the church appearing to have found

her lost serenity. "I learned a big lesson today," she said. "The Father says I'm not to place my trust in those to whom I minister. Rather, I'm to seek His wisdom for each relationship."

She looked down mournfully. "Thomas is not a believer; he's pretending to be one in order to keep his friends. When she lifted her head again, a ray of hope shone from her eyes. "Even so, there's still hope that he will allow God to show him the sin he's been hiding in his heart."

Elaine and I nodded.

"Thank You Father for teaching us Your ways," I said as we hugged Rita.

Chapter 43 – The Thief

On one of my Sabbaths between mission trips, Daniel and I rested on my veranda watching Camelia and Alice flitter joyously among the branches of their golden tree. It appeared that Camelia had found something very special and Alice was taking great pleasure in it.

"I hope Camelia didn't find someone's white stone," I said, wondering what she might have found. "She loves shiny objects."

Daniel was both amused and intrigued by the birds' excitement. "May I go and see what she found?"

"I don't think she would appreciate your looking into her nest." I wanted him to respect her privacy. "If she wanted us to see it, she would show it to us."

"Why would she hide something from us?" he asked looking up at me. "It's not like she stole something." A dubious look crossed his face. "Or did she? Maybe she's a thief."

"No, she didn't steal anything." I felt as though I needed to defend her. I knew she would never deliberately offend the Father. "Maybe she wants to give what she found to someone as a surprise. She often does that."

Daniel seemed satisfied that Camelia's motives were pure. "That's really nice of her." He smiled while watching her.

I knew what had prompted his suspicion. He had been present when my sister Rita told me how someone had stolen valuable items that her singles group had found. It had been no surprise when they found out that the thief was Thomas. His crime had been dealt with swiftly and severely and he'd paid full restitution.

Daniel looked up at me again and said, "I asked the Father if I could have two bird friends as pets and He said I could." Grinning, he added, "I'm going to call them Fred and Felix."

"Those are very nice names for birds. Are you naming them after special people in your life?"

"My two uncles who always gave me treats when my mother took me to see them." He licked his lips.

Catching his intent, I said, "Daniel, would you like some sweet cakes?"

He chuckled, "Oh, yes."

On my way into the house for sweet cakes, I watched Camelia and Alice fly into the sky. I placed a few cakes on a plate and started back to the veranda.

Just then a strong wind from the Mount of Worship buffeted the branches of the golden tree. Camelia's little nest fell to the ground. Daniel went and picked it up. He looked inside before placing it back on its branch.

The wind died down quickly. I put the sweet cakes on a table near Daniel and sat down beside him.

"I saw the breeze blow the nest down. That was unusual."
I didn't say anything about his looking into the nest.

Muffling his voice, he said, "I think your bird friend may
be a thief." I could tell he was honestly trying to be sure
that only I could hear him. "She has two white stones in
her nest; they have writing on them." His implication
ended with a suspicious look in his eye.

"Camelia would not steal anything, Daniel."

He looked at me dubiously for a long moment.

I prayed, *Jesus, I need Your help.*

Daniel noticed someone coming up the footpath and let
out a squeal. "Jesus is coming!" I watched him run to Jesus
as I followed. When he'd almost reached Him, he froze in
mid-step. Camelia and Alice were on Jesus' shoulder.

"Alice and Camelia have a surprise for you, Daniel,"
Jesus told him. He bent down to hug him. The birds flew
over to Camelia's nest and brought it back to Jesus,
managing to carry it between them with their feet.

Jesus took the two stones out of the nest and gave them
to Daniel. "These are what you requested of the Father."

Daniel held them with his hands cupped together. Pointing to one, Jesus said, "This is Fred." Pointing to the other
He said, "And this is Felix." Their names were written on
them.

Jesus smiled while Daniel tried to comprehend the
stones. Daniel looked back and forth between the stones
and Jesus without saying anything.

Jesus then said, "If you're not going to thank the Father
for the stones, they will have to do it for you." He reached
down and touched them. They sparkled with His touch and
we started hearing faint, high-pitched praises and thanksgiving.

Startled by the sounds, Camelia and Alice flew back to
their golden tree with Camelia's nest.

Daniel laughed and said, "Thank You, Jesus." Turning to
the Mount of Worship, he said, "Thank You, Father."

When Daniel looked back at the stones they had grown

quiet and their texture and color had begun to change. They now looked like eggshells. Before long, they cracked open and two chirping birds popped out. Daniel's mouth dropped open.

Jesus laughed heartily. Eventually, Daniel laughed with Him. He cuddled Fred and Felix in his hands while Jesus watched him lovingly.

"Daniel, look at Me." He lifted his chin. "You must thank the Father for all things, even when they don't look like what you asked for. The Father knows what is best for you."

Daniel looked down and nodded.

Fred and Felix, perhaps attracted by Camelia's and Alice's chirping, flew to the golden tree.

Daniel looked up at Jesus very seriously. "I thought Camelia had stolen those white stones."

"I know, Daniel. And because of your suspicion, you were afraid to approach Me."

Daniel nodded again.

Jesus smiled and said, "When such thoughts come to you, ask me about them immediately. I'll give you right thoughts."

The Holy Spirit swept over Daniel in a gentle breeze bringing tears to his eyes.

"I'll apologize to her," he said. He walked over to the golden tree.

Jesus and I watched him apologize and explain. Camelia flew to his shoulder and kissed his cheek.

"I'm glad you're not a thief," Daniel told her.

I started to thank Jesus, but He was already gone. I bent and picked up the cracked eggshells. To my delight, they turned back into two white stones in my hands. Faintly, I could hear them praising and thanking the Father.

"Heaven is so much fun!" I said to the Father. I could hear Him laugh.

Chapter 44 – Visit From a Friend

"Anita! It's so good to see you!" I fought back tears as I hugged her.

Anita repeated "my good friend, my good friend" over and over. Finally, she stood back to look me over. She teased, "You look like you've taken on more of a glow. Heaven has done wonders for you!" She laughed.

"Yes it has," I said joyously. "Come in and visit for a while." I locked her arm in mine and walked her to my door. "Every time I've seen you, you've been on your way to somewhere else. Not today! We must ask the Father if you can spend time with me." I was determined.

With sparkling eyes, she said, "I've already asked; I have so much to tell you."

She stopped short as she entered my parlor, her eyes wide. "Your home, it's so beautiful! Where did you get all the bouquets of flowers?"

"My mother grows flowers for heaven's festivals. You wouldn't believe how big her gardens are."

"They're wonderful! I'd like to get some for my home." She lovingly touched a rose and then stooped to smell an attractive gardenia arrangement. "My, they have a strong fragrance." Her eyes started watering. I had to laugh.

I pulled a chair up for her. "Please, sit down and tell me what you've been doing."

She sat down and took a deep breath. "Where do I start? Well let's see, you know I've been ministering on earth in Arizona, right?"

"Yes."

"Did you know that Arizona's climate really changed after Jesus returned to earth?"

"Yes. I've heard that every nation now has an ideal climate for its region."

She smiled. "I know it doesn't affect resurrected believers much, but it's wonderful for earth-bound people." "Arizona has no blazing deserts anymore. Can you believe it?" She waited for my response.

"Yes, I can believe it. I've heard there aren't any more steaming jungles, either. And the rain forests have pleasant summer weather year-round."

"What about Wisconsin?"

Picturing wonderland scenes of snow-covered pastures, I told her, "They still have snow, but no bitter cold. No one has to worry about frostbite."

"So, what is your ministry in Arizona?" I leaned forward to catch every word.

Her smile transformed into a look of earnestness. "I work with a wonderful group of women. They're all such beautiful Christians. A few are married, but most are single. I know you're aware that people generally marry at a much older age now. Some in my group want to wait until they're a hundred or older before starting their families."

"I've heard that many people will live to be older than the people who lived before the great flood," I replied. "In fact, many who were born before Jesus' coronation will live through the whole thousand years of His reign."

It was hard for us to imagine. "It's amazing!" Anita said enthusiastically. Her face glowed almost as much as her white robe. "Jesus has made the world so clean. Everything people eat and breathe is totally pure." She looked out my window at the Mount of Worship. Breathtaking colors revolved around it like a kaleidoscope. With her face radiating love she said, "Thank You, Jesus."

When she looked back at me, I said, "I haven't seen your daughters Charity and Vicky for some time. "What are they doing?"

A rueful expression fell over her face. "They're working alongside their brothers and sisters in California. She hesitated before adding, "As you know, some of my children had to go through the Tribulation."

Quickly her spirit lifted. "The Father protected them, though. They're all living for Jesus now. We get together often, especially on holidays. Christmas is coming soon, you know."

"In a few months."

She picked up where she'd left off telling me about her children: "We have such unity now! We sit and talk for hours and really enjoy each other's company. What a change from the way it used to be."

"I remember what you said it was like."

A serious look came over her face again as she reminisced. "I knew in my spirit then that the Father had everything under control, but my mind wasn't fully renewed." She stopped to wipe a tear from her eye. "Now, I wonder why I grieved over them so much."

"The renewing of one's mind is difficult, lifelong work," I agreed. "Sorrow was my companion for many years too, until the washing of the Word of God and the power of the Holy Spirit helped me trust the Father with all things. I had to give all my negative thoughts to Him moment-by-moment, and receive His promises. What peace He gives us when we do that!"

I reached over and lovingly touched Anita's hand. "Most of the battle is over for your family now."

She responded through tearful eyes. "Isn't it wonderful to see how God is working in all of us."

We talked at length about what the Father had accomplished in the lives of each of our family members. Afterward, Anita got up and hugged me. "Dear friend, I must leave now. It has been so good talking to you. Promise me you'll come visit me soon, Father willing."

"I promise, Father willing." I walked her to my door. "Stop by my mother's home and get yourself some flowers."

"Okay," she said on her way out." She turned and smiled as she walked down the path. "May the Father bless you."

"He just did," I said waving goodbye.

Chapter 45 -- Children of the Kingdom

"Come, let's go up to the mountain of the Lord, to the house of the God of Jacob. He will teach us His ways so we can walk in His paths."

The prophet Isaiah stood at the foot of the holy mountain dressed in the customary garb of his earthly life. He shouted instructions from under his tallit (tahleet), or Jewish prayer shawl.

Camelia flew excitedly from shoulder to shoulder through the crowd gathered outside Jerusalem to take part in the Advent procession. Isaiah led the procession each year. Everyone followed him slowly up the mountain path listening to his discourse.

"The law will go out from Zion, the Word of the Lord from Jerusalem. He will judge between nations and settle disputes for the peoples."

I looked around at thousands of nationalities gathered in peace. Their weapons had been recast into useful tools and their battle garments had been burned.

I imagined the first Christmas, as I often did during this season. Angels had filled the heavens singing:

Glory to God in the highest,
And peace to men of good will.

This was the peace of the nations of which they had sung.

"Come, O house of Jacob, let us walk in the light of the Lord," Isaiah's voice resounded.

The golden light of the Father began to filter down through a cloud of smoke surrounding the mountain. It bathed the procession's participants in the anointing power of the Holy Spirit. Everyone fell to the ground. Many wept tears of repentance as the Spirit cleansed their hearts.

Soon the light diminished and the people rose to venture up the holy mountain again. Songs of joy filled the air, including several old, familiar Christmas carols.

I joined in one of my favorites:

> *Joy to the world, the Lord is come;*
> *Let earth receive her King.*

These words now had a whole new meaning for the people of earth.

> *Let every heart prepare Him room,*
> *And heaven and nature sing...*

Listening to Camelia sing along brought tears to my eyes.

Jerusalem had been flooded with people for weeks. They were eagerly preparing their hearts for the Feast of Christmas. Many had brought gifts for the Child who had grown to become both a sacrifice and a king. Day and night they climbed the mountain to worship Him.

At night, the whole mountain glowed like flames of fire, giving light to travelers—just like the pillar of fire that guided the ancient Israelites through desert nights. During the day, the Father put a canopy over the mountain to shade the people from the sun and shelter them from rain.

I rejoiced at the climbing masses. *These are the children of the kingdom.* I recognized a few from my missions to earth. Nancy walked beside me and ahead of us Gretchen maneuvered the climb with Elaine's help.

At times, Nancy held my hand. At other times she ran ahead to look for Camelia. I'm sure she wondered why I allowed my "angel bird" to go off on her own. She felt she needed to watch her for me.

This was Gretchen and Nancy's second trip to Jerusalem, their first having been on the occasion of Jesus' coronation. Since this Celebration would continue for four weeks, they would have a chance to visit personally with Jesus.

When everyone had reached the top of the mount, the sky

around the temple grew dark.

"The people walking in darkness have seen a great light," Isaiah shouted to the people.

Jesus walked out of the temple in His glorified form and the light emanating from His body illuminated the mountaintop. Everyone shouted praises to Him. We all fell to our knees to worship Him. Thunder rolled through the heavens above, trailed by a blanket of holy silence.

The Father's voice, sounding like the roar of rushing water, came down from the highest heaven. "My Son reigns on the throne of David! The government is on His shoulders and His Kingdom shall not pass away."

Several choirs of angels assembled into a formation of nine columns in the sky. The columns converged on the center column at their bottom ends to present the image of a gloriously illuminated holiday menorah while the angels sang to their King:

And He is wonderful, counselor, mighty God,
Everlasting Father, Prince of Peace...

The people on the mount remained in deep silence as Jesus smiled down on them. Then, before their eyes, He transformed into His human form so they could approach Him. One by one, two by two, the children of the kingdom met with Jesus, a number of them presenting Him with gifts.

Nancy had made a beautiful doily for Him. When she and I approached Him, He gave us warm hugs before she showed Him the doily. He told her how beautiful it was and how much He appreciated it.

"You can put it on a table in Your home," she suggested.

He smiled affectionately. "Well then, I will have to make a table for My doily."

"I know where You can get some wood," she said with bright eyes.

Jesus laughed. "Someday you must show Me, but for now,

I could wear your gift as My "kippah."

Nancy giggled as He put the crocheted handiwork on His head. I doubt she knew that a kippah was a skullcap worn by Jewish men while they prayed or studied the Torah. It didn't stay on His head long; it fell back into His hand as He bent to hug her. He told her that He would greet her mother next.

As Gretchen and Elaine approached, Jesus blessed me with a resplendent, loving smile.

"My gift was too big to wrap," I told Him teasingly.

"I've heard that before." He laughed.

I had heard Him say many times that we gave Him the best gift of all when we gave Him our total obedience. He said it was pure love and too big to wrap.

With parting smiles, Nancy and I moved aside for Gretchen and Elaine to talk with Jesus. As we navigated to the back of the crowd, I asked Nancy, "Will you and your mother stay in Jerusalem for Christmas?"

"No, we have to go back to the States. Mom said we have relatives there who can't make it to Jerusalem, so we should go and celebrate with them. Where will you celebrate Christmas?"

"Elaine and I will be back in heaven. We'll celebrate with friends and family, and of course with the Trinity."

"That would be so awesome!"

"Yes, it will. Your Christmas celebrations here on earth are wonderful, but those in heaven are absolutely awesome. That's part of the reason they call it heaven."

Nancy laughed and was about to respond when Camelia landed on my head. Nancy scolded her with a frown. "There you are you naughty bird. I was worried about you."

I could feel Camelia flapping her wings strenuously. I knew when her flapping and chirping stopped at intervals that she was bending her head from side to side looking at Nancy. Then she'd start chirping and flapping fretfully again.

"Camelia dear, I'll tell you later what naughty means.

Nancy thinks you need someone to take care of you because you're so small. She loves you; that's why she worries about you."

Camelia flew like lightning to the top of a large rock and sang there nonchalantly for a moment. Then, with just as much speed, she flew back to my head.

Nancy applauded, but I needed to interpret Camelia's demonstration for her.

"Camelia says Jesus takes care of her. He made her able to fly so fast that no one can catch her."

Nancy asked Camelia, "When I'm in heaven, will Jesus make me fly as fast as you?"

Camelia danced on my head. She must have thought she would have a new racing partner.

Elaine and Gretchen joined us. Gretchen was crying softly. She stammered through her tears, "He's so wonderful! I don't think I'll ever be the same!"

"No one is ever the same after meeting Jesus," Elaine confirmed. "Isn't the Christmas Season wonderful!" She laughed as she waltzed around the three of us.

Mother's Christmas Guest List

Dad
Martha
Camelia
Alice

Me
My husband
David
Clint
Travis
Lisa
Rebecca (David's friend)

Elaine
Charles (Elaine's husband)
Char (Elaine's daughter)
Neil (Elaine's son)

Rita
Daryl (Rita's husband)
Jill (Rita's oldest daughter)
Shane (Rita's son)
Holly and Hailly
    (Rita and Daryl's daughters)

Lois
Bill

Chapter 46 – The Christmas Celebration – Part One

Heaven's citizens celebrated the Advent Season while preparing for Christmas, both in heaven and on earth. Though we gave and received many gifts, as the Spirit moved us, Jesus remained the focal point. As Christmas dawned on earth, we gathered in homes of friends and family. Jesus spent His special day with the Father and the Holy Spirit.

The Mount of Worship glowed brilliantly while my husband and I traveled to my mother's home where we would celebrate with my family. Mother was busy in her kitchen with last-minute details when she noticed us coming up the path. She opened her door and called "Merry Christmas."

I was tickled to see that her home had taken on the air of the old-fashioned Christmases I had known on earth. Evergreen boughs accented with gold gossamer garland and crimson and scarlet poinsettias framed each doorway.

She greeted us cheerfully and told us what a joy it had been having Camelia stay for a few hours to help with preparations. Camelia had helped tie gold ribbons donned with tiny silver bells in each window. Martha had felt she needed to help too, so she told Mother and Camelia when each ribbon was positioned correctly.

In spite of Martha's instructions and Camelia's not-too-appreciative responses, they had gotten along well enough to harmonize in Christmas carols as they worked. Though mother hadn't been able to carry a tune during her earthly life, she had a beautiful singing voice in heaven.

"I had a wonderful time," she said, "and no one asked me to just move my mouth and not sing out loud." Her laughter brightened the whole room.

I was already enjoying Christmas at Mother's home. "Is everyone able to come?"

"Your Father is here; Lois and Bill came with him. They're in the family room with Rita and Daryl. Jill and

Shane, Holly and Hailly, and Elaine, Charles and Char are in there too. Elaine said Neil might be a little late. Are all your children able to come?"

"Yes, although they might be a bit late, as well."

I looked around for Martha. "Where's Martha?"

"Jesus asked her to take part in a live nativity scene on earth. Your Father and I celebrated Christmas with her during earth's Christmas Eve."

"Oh, that's wonderful. I'm sure she'll enjoy being in the nativity scene. But I'll miss her."

"She'll be back soon," Mother assured me. She invited my husband and me to join the rest of the family in the family room while she stayed to prepare tables in the dining area. My husband went to greet the others, but I decided to stay and help Mother.

She gave me some deep-blue, silk tablecloths to cover elegantly hand-carved mahogany tables that Dad and Bill had set up earlier. The cushioned seats and backs of the chairs matched the tablecloths. Mother's home was lovely. Elaine and Char had traded hand-fashioned festoons created from evergreen branches cut from the forest around her home for glorious Christmas banners that now hung on her sparkling white walls along with holly and ivy.

Char had given Camelia a little ornament for her golden tree—a small bell with a gold string attached to the hammer. Whenever Camelia pulled the string with her beak, the bell rang out the tune of *Silent Night*. I loved listening to it as often as she played it. Camelia had brought it with her and Mother had placed it atop one of the centerpieces that would decorate our tables.

Camelia had, of course, found a small gift for Char: a shiny white stone. Jesus had written Char's new name on the stone and wrapped it for Camelia, because He was the only One who knew Char's new name. The stone was very precious to Char.

Of all the Christmas items in Mother's home, the one I enjoyed most was a little wooden nativity set which

Charles had hand-carved for her. I had met Jesus' mother, Mary, and His stepfather, Joseph. I'd also met some of the shepherds that visited the manger that first Christmas. The likeness of the little figurines to the real people was uncanny. The exactness was even more astounding given that Charles had never carved wood while he lived on earth. I asked him how he'd learned to carve so beautifully and make them look so realistic. He looked at me in the same way Camelia would—slightly bending his head to one side with a smile.

"Jesus taught me."

I should have guessed.

Camelia also loved the little nativity set, especially the baby Jesus. She listened carefully each time I told her the Christmas story. She had talked with Jesus about it recently and afterward had asked Mother if she could take the baby Jesus and show him to her friends. Mother had consented thinking it was cute. But the baby was seldom in the manger after that. I'd asked Camelia to be sure to have the figurine in the manger on Christmas morning. Looking down at the sweet baby, I was glad she had remembered.

The doorbell rang and my husband, having returned to look for me, opened the door. He smiled back at Mother and me saying, "We have someone who appears to be an angel at our door." Shane heard him from the family room and came running to see who it was.

Neil stood at the door with a handmade halo on his head and a pair of gossamer wings draped over his shoulders.

"And what are you supposed to be?" Shane asked him rubbing his chin, pretending to give the halo's meaning great deliberation.

Neil raised his arm and extended his index finger upward to proclaim, "I am an angel come to bring you good news: Lisa, Dave, Rebecca, Clint and Travis are walking through the forest at this moment and will soon cross the footbridge." Shane and I looked down the path and saw them coming.

"I see that you are a prophetic angel," Shane teased.

"Neil, you have a wonderful sense of humor," I said, and gestured for him to come in.

By this time, everyone had come to the door to see an "angel." Char asked her brother, "Where did you get the halo?"

"From a young girl on earth. She said she would feel real hurt if I didn't wear it."

"A little girl who thinks you're an angel?" Shane quipped.

Neil smiled and took it off. "Now I have worn it for her. Here, Grandma."

Mother took the halo and welcomed him with a hug. "Thank you. I will use it." She handed it to Rita.

Rita and Lois thought it would go well as a table centerpiece, so Lois lifted a vase of flowers and Rita placed the halo in the center of the table. Then Lois replaced the flowers in the middle of the halo. "Perfect," they said in unison.

Rita spread out the flowers and said, "This will be your table, Mother." Mother smiled.

Shane continued to tease Neil as they browsed the buffet table. "I'm sure you have broken a little heart by taking it off."

When Lisa, Rebecca and my sons arrived, we were ready to sit down to a sumptuous Christmas dinner to be topped off with plum pudding.

After all were seated, Dad lifted his glass of new wine and said, "I would like to make a toast to the Father, to Jesus and to the Holy Spirit, in gratefulness for Their making it possible for us to celebrate Christmas in heaven." We raised our glasses and took a drink of wine.

Brother-in-law Bill raised his glass next in a toast, "I would like to toast all of our sons and daughters and brothers and sisters on earth who will join us in time." His stepson Carl and stepdaughter Mary (Lois' children) were still on earth.

After Bill's toast, Holly raised her glass with a bright

"Happy Birthday Jesus!" Hailly repeated the gesture: "Happy Birthday Jesus!" One by one we followed their example. Then, while we ate, we told stories of past Christmases in heaven.

Chapter 46 – The Christmas Celebration – Part Two

I'll never forget my first Christmas in heaven," Lisa began. "Everything was so glorious! I couldn't stop crying on my way up the Mount of Worship. I cried every time I saw Jesus that first season."

"I remember," David said, shaking his head. He turned and told Rebecca, "We had to keep taking her to the Sacred River until she finally started carrying some of its water around with her in a jar." He turned back and smiled at Lisa. "You haven't changed much, Sis."

"I couldn't help it. Everything was so perfect and I was so happy. Although, I do remember telling Camelia that, in spite of everything, I still missed snow at Christmas. Camelia told Jesus and, sure enough, snow started falling. But it wasn't normal snow."

"Nothing is exactly normal in heaven," Travis interjected.

Lisa gloried in her memories. "It was white and soft and sparkled like diamonds. It wasn't too cold, just cold enough to be fun and bring back memories of earth."

"And the weather!" Clint gloried with her. "It wasn't anything like the Wisconsin winter weather I remember from my childhood!"

"We made snowballs and snowmen," Neil broke in, caught up in their exuberance.

"After you stood there forever just watching it come down," Shane ribbed him.

Char said, "I remember we made angels in the snow." She raised and lowered her arms pretending they were wings.

"And we made a snowball so big," Travis jumped up to show its size, "that we needed an angel to help us roll it."

David asked him, "Do you remember the angel telling us how he and some other angels had made snowballs and thrown them down on the Amorites, Israel's enemies? He told us they pressed the snow so hard that they were actually huge hailstones." We could tell he was still fascinated by the story.

Clint added, "Scripture says more Amorites died from the hailstones than from the swords of Israel."

"It was such a beautiful gift!" Lisa said. By all appearances, she had not heard a word anyone else had spoken. She'd been enthralled in the memory of Jesus' gift of snow that first Christmas.

About that time, Camelia flew into the room and landed on my head. "Camelia," Rita called from the next table, "did you hang all these beautiful ribbons with the bells?" Camelia chirped proudly and flew to a window to demonstrate how she had put them up. Moving her head up and down, she took her bow while we clapped.

"They're very beautiful," Jill told her. "You and Alice must come and visit me someday soon."

"Where is Alice?" Lois asked, not wanting to be surprised. Alice always seemed to fly right for her head.

Camelia chirped a response and I interpreted: "Alice is coming with some of her friends." Lois' face went peaked. Rita laughed and her little daughters clapped.

We had just finished eating when numerous birds came in through the windows and circled the room flying from person to person. Lois ducked and covered her head with her hands. Bill tried to keep the birds away from her. Alice flew right to her head and landed on her hands. She looked down at her with a "What's the matter?" look.

"Camelia," Lois called, "perhaps you should entertain your friends in your golden tree." Many of my relatives nodded in agreement. Only Holly and Hailly seemed to really enjoy the birds. Daryl and Shane tried to keep the girls from getting too rambunctious. Rita and Jill looked as though they were enjoying watching the girls more than the birds.

In the midst of all the confusion, Camelia flew to the top of the nativity scene and chirped authoritatively. The other birds settled down. When she finished, it was my turn.

"It seems Camelia has taken the carving of the baby Jesus around to all her friends telling them about the Christmas story. Now they all want to hear the story." I gave my relatives my most pleading expression.

A breeze of the Holy Spirit blew through the room softening hearts.

"Papa Louie, would you do the reading," Mother asked Dad, handing him the Bible.

He ushered us to the sitting room where he had started a fire in the hearth. It crackled and sang in a brilliant display of dancing flames, and gave only enough warmth to elicit ooohhs and ahhhs. We nestled on soft chairs or the luxurious white wool carpet and waited for Dad to begin.

Rita asked Holly and Hailly to refrain from playing with the birds so they could listen to the story. Shane took one of the girls on his lap and Jill took the other. The birds remained silent while Dad opened the book.

In those days, Caesar Augustus issued a decree
That a census should be taken of the entire Roman
world.

As Dad started reading, an anointing of the Holy Spirit filled the room. We wept softly as the Spirit made that first Christmas real for us. We could hear angelic voices singing.

Glory to God in the highest and peace to His people on earth.

As the story continued, my thoughts slipped away to loved ones still on earth. I wondered how they were celebrating Jesus' birthday.

When Dad closed the book, all the birds flapped their wings and flew around the room. Bill quickly put a pillow over Lois' head. After circling the room a few times, the birds flew out the windows, ringing the bells as they left. Holly and Hailly jumped up and down giggling and clapping.

"Did Camelia plan that?" Neil asked me.

"I don't know if she planned it or not, Neil, but ringing the bells in praise to the Lord was certainly a fitting response to the story." I lifted my hands in praise.

"They're flying toward the Mount of Worship," Shane commented looking out the window. "They're probably going to talk to the Father and Jesus about the story."

Rita and Daryl said, "Praise the Lord!" together.

"We can all take a lesson from those birds," I suggested, "and end our celebration with praise." Rita started a Christmas carol and soon we were all singing praises with God's love flooding our hearts.

We hugged one another when we finished.

"Another wonderful Christmas in our memories," Elaine whispered as we hugged.

"I think we'll remember this Christmas for some time," Travis said squeezing me.

"You have a feather on your head." Clint reached over and flicked it off.

Rebecca asked, "Hadn't the birds heard the Christmas story before?"

David nodded, thinking they must have.

"They'd probably heard it many times," I agreed. "But I think when they saw the tiny figure of Jesus, they may have realized for the first time just how little He had become for mankind."

We all looked at the nativity scene.

"He was even smaller than that in the womb," Rebecca pointed out, appearing deep in thought.

"I told Camelia that," I said, "but she just kept repeating, "He was smaller than me!"

Elaine said, "I guess the birds have a new awareness of how much Jesus loves us."

Daryl added, "Seems to have made a deep impression on them."

I walked to the window and looked out at the Mount of Worship. "Thank You, Jesus," I whispered, brushing a tear from my cheek. I turned back to see Charles showing the baby Jesus to Holly and Hailly, and smiled.

Chapter 47 -- Mother's Orphan

990 years later . . .

O beautiful for spacious skies,
For amber waves of grain,
For purple mountains majesty
Above the fruited plains.
America, America,
God shed His grace on thee.
And crowned thy good with brotherhood
From sea to shining sea.

Mother sang as we gazed at the snow-covered mountains of Montana. With her heavenly ability to sing well, a cappella songs accompanied us whenever we traveled together. And we had been traveling a lot lately.

On this trip, she had asked the Father if we could visit her children in Wisconsin and the Father had allowed us to visit my sister Jean, in Florida, and my brother Bill, in Minnesota, as well.

Mother sang her patriotic song with her heart filled with joy. After finishing the last stanza, she squeezed my hand softly and said, "It's such a blessing to know all my children are doing fine."

"It was good to see the nieces and nephews and their children too."

We were on the mission leg of our journey, entering Helena high in the Rockies.

"That used to be a cancer research center." Mother pointed to an old opaque glass building. "Now it's full of craft shops and bartering markets."

"I remember when most of the medical practitioners needed to learn new professions after Jesus eradicated all of the diseases like cancer, heart disease and diabetes. I still can't imagine even childbearing quick and painless."

At the mention of cancer, the light in Mother's eyes dimmed and her face contorted. "Cancer was a terrible disease."

I put my arm around her and agreed. "It was an awful way to die, Mother." She looked down and shook her head.

When she looked up again, she smiled and said, "I did get to spend more time in heaven than the rest of you." I smiled.

"Where are we going again?" she asked.

"Jesus asked us to visit a family that's experiencing some domestic and social problems. A young girl has been praying for her parents who want to be free from Jesus' rule. Sickness of the body may have been eliminated, but there are still a lot of people who are sick in their souls."

Mother was shocked. "We saw what a mess the world was in before Jesus' return—when everyone did as they pleased."

"That was almost a thousand years ago, Mother. Most citizens of earth were born during Jesus' reign and they have no memory of what it was like."

"Surely they've heard."

"They've chosen not to believe."

"That's madness!"

"I agree. Look, here's their home." I pointed to a large Victorian house in a row of similar homes. It hadn't taken long to find it; Jesus' directions are always perfect.

We knocked on the door and a tall man with dark, ominous eyes regarded us through a porch window but didn't open the door. I opened it myself.

"We don't need your help," he snarled, trying to shut the door and keep us from entering.

I held it open with supernatural strength and told him, "We need to talk." Seething with anger, he stepped back.

His wife appeared from an inner room. Her eyes narrowed in distrust when she saw us. "Please be seated," she said, forcing a smile. She moved some books and papers from chairs so we could sit. The home was untidy, but clean enough. The two sat down on their couch facing us.

I introduced Mother and myself and then told them why we were there. "We're not here to harass you," I said. Although, there are some things you must do to have peace and harmony at your workplace and in your community."

Hatred smoldered in the man's eyes. He clenched his fists. I watched his knuckles turn white from pressure.

"All your rules and regulations are smothering me," he muttered under his breath. Glaring at me, he said, "I will be free!" His wife moved slightly away from him. I sensed her fear.

"May we visit with your daughter Kelsey?" I asked politely.

"You leave our daughter alone!" He jumped up and grabbed my arm to pull me to my feet. I stood, but then freed myself from his grip and pushed him away. The look on his face told me that he just then realized he couldn't hurt me.

"We'll leave now," I said. "However, we may visit again."

After his wife showed us to the door civilly, he slammed it shut when we'd barely made it through the doorway.

"He has no understanding of the wonderful freedom found in Christ," I said to Mother.

Angry over the way he'd treated us, she said loud enough for the couple to hear: "Freedom from the anger and hatred that consumes him." She said more quietly as we stepped down the porch steps, "What about the woman?"

"Jesus said He's working in her heart. She hasn't hardened it completely—at least not yet." I looked back to see if either were watching us and caught a curtain closing.

"Surely the girl is under divine protection," Mother said. I'd like to see him try to tackle her angel." Her anger had subsided and her face had taken on a confident, but still almost smug, look. "He needs to give his anger to Jesus."

With our mission completed, we went back to heaven and wasted no time telling everyone how the rest of our family on earth was doing. Involved in our duties and other missions, we soon all but forgot the little girl and her family.

Months later, while we worked in Mother's gardens, Jesus visited us.

"Peace be with you, My sisters."

He smiled as we rose excitedly to greet Him. But then sadness came over His face and He remorsefully told us what had taken place just a few weeks previous at the couple's home. The man had beaten his wife to death. A loving Christian couple had taken their daughter Kelsey in.

"Would you go back to earth and help Kelsey adjust to her new family."

"My poor little orphan girl," Mother grieved with tears welling up in her eyes.

"The Father's children are never orphans," Jesus corrected her.

The Holy Spirit ministered comfort and strength to her and she said, "We'll go help her adjust."

Jesus thanked us warmly. He looked at the flowers we tended and thanked us again for our good and patient work.

Mother picked a sky-blue blossom in the shape of a cloud and presented it to Him. He took it and then with a glorious smile and a nod, He was gone.

Arriving at Kelsey's new home, we found that, although she was not able to smile yet, she was adjusting well. Wanting to comfort her, Mother took her for a walk in the garden.

While watching Kelsey and Mother relating to each other, I talked with Kelsey's new parents about their needs. Everything appeared to be in order and Kelsey seemed relaxed talking to Mother and picking flowers. She gave Mother a hesitant smile. Mother held her close for a moment.

"I know Kelsey will be happy here," I told the couple.

Her new father responded emotionally: "We feel that she is a precious gift—one we will always treasure."

Just then, Kelsey came running in from the garden and shyly presented her new mother with a small bouquet of flowers. Tears came to the woman's eyes. Mother came in and she and I watched the bonding of this precious new family until we sensed it was time to go.

After we left, Mother sang "America the Beautiful" again. I pondered the lyrics and thought, *Yes, it's through Jesus' grace that this new family is crowned with brotherhood.*

Mother stopped singing and looked at me. She said, "Even the most beautiful of places can be ugly when sin is in it."

Understanding that she spoke of America, I said, "Yes, but brotherhood like that of Kelsey's new family can make it shine beautifully again."

She commenced her singing with greater fervor. Light shone from her eyes as she sang, "God shed His grace on thee."

Though sin had grown deep roots in some hearts over time, America was, indeed, still beautiful.

Chapter 48 -- Bird in a Trap

It had been quite a while since the last time Elaine and I had gone on a mission together. We compared notes on our recent missions in her kitchen over a meal of tender vegetables and dried fruit. Updating me on her family, she told me about Char and Jill's latest episode while on furlough from a shared mission on earth:

"Come and look," Char yelled. "There's a bird in a trap over here!"

Jill ran over to see. "How do you suppose that happened in heaven?" She disbelieved what she saw.

The cousins were on their way to my mother's home for a visit and had been discussing some difficulties they were experiencing with a few of their relationships on earth. Char had run ahead to beat Jill to the footbridge and had almost run into a wire trap.

"The bird isn't really trapped," She told Jill. "See, the door is open. How odd!" She knelt down and urged the bird to come out. "Come out little bird."

"You may need to reach in and pull her out." Jill advised.

Char reached into the trap, but quickly pulled her hand back when the little fledgling pecked at her fingers. "Don't do that!" she scolded.

"She can't hurt you," Jill laughed.

"Well, birds aren't supposed to be in traps in heaven either, but here it is." Char stood and put her hands on her hips.

"I'll try." Jill knelt down and reached into the trap. The bird repeatedly flew away from her hand. "She's fast! She must be the same kind of bird as Camelia." She stood and stared down at the feathered creature along with Char.

Eventually, the two decided to sit by the bank of the stream and think about what they might try next.

Dipping her fingers in the cool water, Jill said, "This reminds me of our friends on earth. They think the new things they want to try are so great. They don't realize they'll end up trapped just like this bird." She got up and went back to the wire cage for another look.

Thinking out loud, Char said, "The same way *we* were once trapped in our lifestyles on earth.

"Exactly," Jill said. "The doors of our cages were open too. But just like this little gal, we didn't want to come out."

"There was a feeling of security in there."

"Right, and when people reached in to help us out, we got angry and did everything we could to avoid them, just like her." Jill had been staring at the little bird in bewilderment, but now she came back to Char and sat beside her.

"So how do we help our friends?" Char asked. She bent her knees so she could rest her elbows on them while she cradled her head in the palms of her hands.

"Are you out trapping birds today?" someone called from the path on the other side of the stream. They looked up to see Neil approaching the footbridge.

"I saw the two of you sitting here and had to come over to investigate." Spotting the bird in the wire cage, he said, "Just as I suspected, you're up to no good."

"It isn't funny, Neil" Jill complained.

Neil sat down next to the girls. "No, it isn't. I don't think Jesus likes what you're doing to that poor bird."

"Neil," Char said impatiently, "we found the bird that way. We're trying to get it out, but it won't come."

"Ah! A rebel bird!"

Char gave him a withering glance. "Little brothers are hard to take even in heaven."

Jill related to Neil how they'd been talking about their earthly friends who wanted to try things that would get them as trapped as the bird.

"Ah," Neil said. "Is it the 'morals of our times are old-fashioned' or the 'I want to have fun' syndrome?"

"Maybe both," Char said looking serious.

"Well how did the two of you get out of your traps on earth?" The girls looked at each other.

Jill was about to speak when they heard footsteps on the bridge. "Jesus!" She jumped up and ran to meet Him. Char and Neil followed.

Jesus hugged each of them. Looking at them lovingly, He said, "I heard you have a problem here." He looked deep into their hearts.

"We have a bird in a trap." Char pointed to the trap.

"We also need to know how to minister to some friends on earth," Jill added, hanging on to Jesus' arm as they walked over to the trap.

Jesus looked down at the caged bird. "This bird has surrendered all of her heavenly freedoms and privileges." He looked back at the three. "The Holy Spirit will continue to urge her to come out. Perhaps Our love may move her to desire heavenly fellowship, or perhaps missing the comforts or spiritual food of heaven will bring her out. But the decision belongs to the bird. If she wants to stay in her trap, her heart will remain in the trap even if you manage to pull her out." He looked deep into the hearts of the cousins again.

"For this bird, and for your friends, do whatever the Holy Spirit tells you. That way we will all be working together to free those we love."

"Thank You, Jesus," the three responded.

Jesus looked at Neil and said, "I have a mission for you, Neil. Would you walk with Me while I explain it to you."

"Of course."

Jesus said goodbye to Char and Jill before putting His arm around Neil's shoulder and walking with him over the bridge.

Elaine's story ended prematurely when she saw Char coming up the path toward her home. "Here comes Char now!" She got up to meet her at the door.

"How's it going with your friends on earth?" I asked Char before taking a bite of an apple and then holding one out to her.

"Thank you," she said taking it. "We told them the lesson of the trap. Mother told you about that?"

"Yes, she was just telling me the story."

"Well, some of them decided to trust Jesus and live by His guidance." With trembling voice, she added, "Others went their own way and are beginning to experience the consequences."

"It's been almost a thousand years since the people of earth had a real taste of God's wrath," I said. "This rebellion was prophesied."

"Yes," she said, her voice still trembling, "but it's difficult when it's people you love."

Elaine and I looked at each other with mutual looks of understanding.

Char sat down at the table and ate with us in silence. All at once, she looked up with a glimmer in her eye and said,

"The Father just told me to give my burden to Him." She didn't have to tell us she had already done just that.

I asked, "What happened to the bird?"

"We never saw it again. Maybe it wasn't actually there. Maybe it was a vision. This is heaven after all!"

Chapter 49 -- Leaf in the Wind

"Hello, Rebecca, I hope you don't mind my dropping by."

"Oh, hello! Come in." Rebecca came to her terrace with a pleasant smile and warm hug.

She led me into her home with her arm around mine.

"I was just praying that you would stop by. Thank You, Father," she said looking up. Her large brown eyes smiled. I had a special love for my son's dear friend.

"I just baked some bread; would you like some?"

My mouth started watering. "Most definitely."

She cut two thick slices and spread them lightly with honey butter. We sat down at her sculptured marble table to enjoy them.

"This is delicious!"

"Thank you. I find food much more enjoyable in heaven than it was on earth, don't you?" She took a big bite and hummed, "Yum!"

"How would you like to see a beautiful part of heaven that you have never seen before, Rebecca?"

She looked at me doubtfully. "With as much as David and I love to travel, I thought we'd seen all of heaven—not that we ever tire of any of it."

"Well, you haven't seen this place yet. Would you like to?"

"I'll ask the Father." She raised her eyes toward the Mount of Worship.

Looking back at me, she said, "The Father says I can go."

A breeze of the Holy Spirit picked us up and floated us away, still enjoying our bread.

Before long, we heard a familiar voice. "Hello." Travis said, floating past us with his angelic guardian.

"Hi," we called back. "Where are you headed?"

"To visit David on earth."

I hollered, "say hello to him for us," as the distance between us grew.

He yelled back, "Will do," before he passed out of our sight.

Floating over the Golden Sea, we saw the whale playing in his favorite spot. I pointed to the rock I had been stranded on, still covered with vegetation, and was about to share my adventure with Rebecca when she said, "David told me about your adventure with the whale and the rock. I don't think I could enjoy waves almost washing me off a rock."

"It wasn't much fun," I admitted, "but it was very meaningful."

I pointed again when we passed over the Valentine Garden. She said, "The garden is an extraordinarily wonderful place. David has taken me there many times." Her face beamed.

I confided, "It's my favorite place in all of heaven, after the Throne Room, of course."

We had reached the mountains. The Spirit gently set us down at the base of the tallest ridge. We feasted our eyes on the snow-covered peak. Shimmering water fell from rocks just below the snow line into a clear stream that ran by the place we stood.

Looking downstream, we noticed a deer decked with a huge rack of antlers drinking at the river's bank a short distance from us.

"It's so beautiful! You were right. I have never seen this place before." She walked over to pet the deer. He cordially met her halfway. When she stopped petting him, he nuzzled her hand in appreciation.

"You are so sweet. What's your name?" The deer just looked at her.

"Not all of heaven's animals talk," I reminded her, strolling over to pet the deer.

She looked around and commented on how the land looked barren and dry. "It's strange to see a waterfall here. Did you notice that the water has a silver tint?"

Before I could answer, she said, "That's what we should call the deer: Silver."

"Well, Silver," I said, "we've just met you, but Rebecca and I need to leave."

I told Rebecca, "I would like you to meet a woman who lives near here."

She lovingly stroked Silver's neck a few more times before walking with me back to the mountain path. She didn't ask who we were going to see; she loves surprises.

We followed the pathway halfway to the crest before coming to a high stone wall with an archway so low and narrow that we needed to crawl through it. Rebecca gazed all around on the other side of the wall. She didn't want to miss any of the mountain's features. In a cleft of the mountain, we found a lush green meadow. Across the meadow, partially hidden by towering trees and flowering shrubs, stood a delightful hewn-rock home. We could smell the fragrant flowers surrounding it. They made the dwelling an aromatic scene of rare beauty.

Rebecca released a gasp of pleasure, "A mountain oasis!"

"Isn't it inspiring! I breathed. Makes one want to break out in praise." I raised my hands in praise to the Father.

Rebecca followed me up the narrow footpath to the door of the home. When I pulled a string attached to a small bell, a beautiful woman with dark hair and light skin came to the door. She wore a graceful veil of silver sheen that flowed over her white robe much like the waterfall flowed over the mountainside. She looked a lot like Rebecca.

Her eyes sparkled as she hugged us and invited us in. "You must be Rebecca," she said to Rebecca. "The Father told me you would visit. My name is Rebekah, also. Your friend David has worked with my Isaac a number of times."

Rebecca's chin dropped. "You're Isaac's Rebekah?" Rebekah nodded. The two women embraced affectionately. Then Isaac's Rebekah gave me another amiable welcoming squeeze as well.

Rebecca said, "It is so good to meet you! David tells me all the time about working alongside Isaac. I can't believe I'm in your house!" She laughed nervously.

Rebekah's home was breathtakingly beautiful. She led us to an expansive parlor that opened to a garden with a flowing stream and motioned for us to have a seat on exquisitely hand-embroidered linen cushions that circled a low table. Surrounded by magnificent pillars ornately decorated with rare jewels, we talked about many things, including our families.

When we spoke of our children, Rebekah's face waxed more serious. "It seems that things are once again getting difficult for families on earth—even with Jesus as Ruler. Isaac has had numerous problems maintaining godly environments for children in all of his territories. David may have told you about some of the new obstacles particular to his region." Rebecca didn't respond. She appeared to have gone deep into thought.

Rebekah poured drinks of fresh-pressed pomegranate juice for us and positioned a plate of date cakes on the table in front of us.

Rebecca didn't notice. I knew she was still thinking about the arising hardships on earth. The situation was too difficult for her to bear.

"I wish there were something I could do to help," she said. "I've asked the Father and He's told me that He has everything under control. Still, I'm tempted to speak with David's adversaries. They're only human; I'm not afraid of them. One way or the other, I feel that I can somehow make them see their error, make them be more reasonable."

"I understand how you feel," Rebekah said. "When Isaac was going to give Esau his blessing rather than Jacob, I felt that way, too, and I took matters into my own hands. God had promised that the older son would serve the younger, but I couldn't wait for God. Do you know what happened?"

"Yes," Rebecca said, "Jacob got the blessing."

"Yes, he did get the blessing," Rebekah's eyes lowered. "but I was not blessed."

Rebecca looked confused.

Tears filled Rebekah's eyes as she explained, "I lost both of my sons that day: I never saw Jacob again on earth after he ran from Esau's fury. And I lost Esau's respect, not to mention my husband's, for a long, long time. She took Rebecca's hand gently in hers and told her, "When we take matters into our own hands by doing things the Father has not asked us to do, we become like leaves in the wind. We're blown about wherever the winds of life scatter us." She smiled sweetly and told her, "God wants us to remain as solid rocks in Him."

Rebecca's face brightened with understanding. "Jesus told David that he was a rock, a rock that stood on Him— the Immovable Rock. He told him that as long as he remained standing on Him the winds and waves of adversity could not move him."

"And you also, Rebecca, must trust the Father to take care of the difficult situations on earth." Rebekah took Rebecca's hand comfortingly and asked, "Would you like to see the gardens the Father has given to me and Isaac?"

Rebecca gave her a broad smile. "That would be wonderful!"

We all rose and walked the grounds enjoying the gardens'

sublime beauty while chatting and sharing our hearts. All too soon, it was time to leave.

Isaac's Rebekah invited us to come again. "If the Father wills, you must promise me you will visit again."

We promised.

A breeze of the Spirit floated us out of the meadow toward the Golden Sea. Deep peace rested on Rebecca's face as she watched the land passing below us.

"Thank you for taking me there," she sighed. "I needed to hear everything Rebekah said."

Chapter 50 -- A Brother in Need

Soon Satan would be loosed. He loitered at his prison door waiting for the moment. The armies of heaven had trained for the ensuing battle and were well prepared. Soldiers and angels would guard heaven's citizens when they traveled to earth, or anywhere accessible to Satan's forces.

Dad and Martha had been asked to haul water from the Sacred River to the training fields again. The Father had asked me to help them when the armies began their final drills.

"Just like the good ol' days," Martha recited in a western drawl. Dad was amused by her earthly comments. He stroked her neck. Her lips curled up in a wide smile. "Yes, it feels good to put in a full day's work: gives one a feeling of accomplishment. A donkey's self-worth comes from a job well done." She stopped rambling and looked at Dad.

Dad regarded her for a moment. "Where did you get all that?"

"Just a few things I picked up on earth." She brayed a long bray and then let out a loud guffaw. "That's a little donkey humor for you." Dad just looked at her. "So how about a little Louie humor?"

"Conversing with a donkey all day is humorous enough for me."

The three of us walked on toward the training fields. Just before we reached them, Martha started up again. She had a question for Dad: "Have you ever noticed that humans laugh at the strangest things? For instance, if someone trips and falls, a human laughs. But a donkey laughs when someone trips and doesn't fall."

Dad smirked. "Why do you suppose that is?"

"I think donkeys have a more sophisticated sense of humor." That brought a hearty laugh from Dad. Martha eyed him curiously. Dad patted her head and continued down the path.

When we arrived at the training fields, I helped Dad pour water into containers near the edge of the fields. As I worked, I searched the soldiers' faces for anyone I might recognize and eventually spotted Shane.

"Dad, I'm going to visit Shane, sitting over there under that tree." I pointed. Dad nodded.

Martha lifted her head high and brayed, "Don't be too long now. You know how I worry about you."

I hugged her. "I love you, Martha; I won't be long."

Shane was surprised to see me on the field and got up eagerly to greet me with a hug. When he sat back down under the tree, I joined him. He didn't offer any conversation.

Noticing Dad and Martha talking to some soldiers, I said, "I wonder if Martha really understands everything she says?"

"Sure she understands," Shane returned. "She's smarter

than all the rest of us put together."

I said, "I don't know if I like the idea of a donkey being smarter than I." Wary of his comeback, I quickly changed the subject. "How is the training coming?"

"The angel who's training me works me right into the ground."

"Shane, you're as bad as Martha with your earthly sayings. Is that why you're sitting here while the others are practicing?"

"No, it's not. Zebulum was called away on a mission. He'll be back soon enough. In the meantime, I will rest." He leaned back against the tree.

"Zebulum? He's not the Zebulum assigned to the city Travis will govern, is he?"

He whispered, "That's right."

I quieted my voice too. "You can't talk about it?"

In his normal voice he said, "Sure. I'm just building suspense for you." He pretended to sleep again.

I feigned agitation saying, "How did your mother put up with you for so many years?"

Shane jolted straight up with a startled look and said, "I don't want to be responsible for your anger;"—I detected a twinkle in his eye—"so I'll tell you. Zebulum and I will guard Travis when Satan and his armies are released. I will be your son's babysitter, so to speak."

That was a sobering thought. I must have had an incredulous expression.

"Seriously," Shane said, "without the armies of heaven, very little godly work would get done on earth."

"I hate to think of what's ahead," I gulped.

We lapsed into silence while watching soldiers maneuver battle stances on the field.

"Ah, Zebulum is back." Shane rose to meet him. He was unmistakably a warrior angel, tall and powerful, a glistening sword strapped at his side.

I stood to meet him when Shane introduced me. He seemed genuinely pleased to meet Travis' mother.

I unwittingly stared at his sword. It was the largest sword I had ever seen. Smiling down at me, he patted it and said, "I've been keeping your son safe."

Shane started joking with Zebulum about Travis. "He is most certainly a brother in need. 'I need. I need. I need,' that's all he ever says."

Zebulum grasped Shane's shoulders and gave him an iron stare. Speaking to me, he said, "Working with Shane will take a great deal of supernatural grace on my part."

Shane looked away and noticed Dad and Martha coming toward us. "Grandpa and Martha are coming. I sure could use some sacred water before we begin mortal combat again."

Zebulum looked for Dad and Martha to verify Shane's claim and released his shoulders when he spotted them. Shane started down the grassy bluff to meet Dad and Martha.

"Mortal combat?" I repeated to Zebulum.

"He's afraid I'll kill him while teaching him how to stay in one piece."

I grinned, but then more seriously asked, "When you fight demonic forces, since neither you nor the demons can die, what do you accomplish?"

Zebulum answered thoughtfully: "The demons' main goal is to keep God's servants from accomplishing their godly missions. They use whatever means they have to hinder the saints. It's our job to protect flesh and blood believers and pre-believers from harm, and to create environments in which their missions can be accomplished."

We watched Shane dialogue with Martha and Dad as they walked our way. Martha joked, "I need, I need, I need." Her braying laugh echoed through the valley.

"Laughter is medicine for the soul," I said to Zebulum.

Smiling lovingly, he agreed. "Very troublesome days are ahead for the rulers of earth. Even those with quick wit like your son Travis will be tempted by negative thoughts and may allow themselves to become stressed or depressed.

Problems, as you know, have a way of causing us to focus on them rather than on Jesus. Humor has a way of helping us keep our eyes off of our problems. Shane's humor will place him as a brother needed by many."

Shane, Dad and Martha joined us, but it was time for Shane and Zebulum to return to the fields. As they marched out, Shane shouted back, "Back to the rudiments of warfare."

"Yes, and I must get back to work. A donkey's work is never done." With uplifted head, Martha picked up her soliloquy and walked ahead of Dad and me toward the path leading home.

Dad and I smiled. It would be an enjoyable trip home.

Chapter 51 -- Satan Is Loosed

Flags flew at half-staff while church bells mourned continual dirges. This was a day of great distress for earth's citizens, intensified by foreboding black clouds shrouding the world. Birds and animals kept silent, seemingly aware of Satan's imminent release. Satan and his demonic followers would be set free from the Abyss this day.

I joined Rita to support her missionary work during this time. Her singles group had asked her to speak to them about what they could expect. She oriented me while we walked to the hotel where she would speak.

"The people are fearful and depressed. We need to

encourage them," she said.

We heard agitated voices as we neared the meeting room. Silence fell when we entered. Rita walked to the podium and looked out at familiar faces. I selected a front-row seat near the wall and sat to listen.

"I'm here to encourage you," she began, "and to help you know what you can expect in the days ahead. What you need to keep in mind is that God the Father and Jesus your ruler are still in complete control." Sighs of relief were audible. "Angels and heavenly soldiers are positioned in every city in the world." Her listeners appeared to relax a little. "Satan will not attack earth or its inhabitants. He will come as an angel of light, an ambassador of freedom. He will gain his followers by deception." All eyes were on Rita.

She quizzed the group: "What can you do to be able to recognize his lies?"

A frail woman in the front row raised her hand.

"Yes," Rita said.

"We can read the Scriptures and make sure we understand them."

"Very good. The Holy Spirit is teaching you." She addressed the group again, asking, "What else must we do besides read the Word and understand it?"

A hand in the back went up.

"Yes," she responded to a young man.

"We must believe it." He spoke with conviction.

"Excellent! You need not fear if only you believe God's Word and never forget that Jesus loves you."

I looked around and saw many tears of conviction falling.

"What else must we do?" Rita looked out at seeking eyes. After waiting a few moments, she said, "We must all pray daily. Spend as much time as possible talking to the Father and Jesus. And, we must always obey the Holy Spirit."

She opened the podium to questions and answered several before the crowd dispersed. After the last person said goodbye, angels escorted Rita and I back to her suite.

From there we would be transported back to heaven.

I posed a question to her while we walked: "I wonder if some of these people remember *how* to pray."

"Things have been so good for so long for them," she sighed.

"Hundreds of years for most," I pointed out. They still have their sin natures, and may have grown lazy in their spiritual walk." I stopped walking and waited for her response.

She stopped and nodded. "Many don't reach out to God unless they're in trouble or need. Earth has been trouble-free for so long that they've forgotten about pleasing God and live only to please themselves." Her expression reflected her deeply saddened spirit as she spoke the dismal words: "Many people are ripe for Satan's lies."

"Yes," I said, sorrowfully.

The moment we were transported back to heaven I took a deep breath of celestial air. Immediately, a sense of peace and wellbeing filled my heart. Looking toward the Mount of Worship, I could tell Jesus was talking with the Father. How I loved that magnificent swirling spectrum of colors. "It's so good to be home!" My heart danced with joy.

"What a contrast!" Rita burst out in a laugh. I watched the glory of the Father settle on her face while I felt the sensation of its settling on me. Trying to hold back tears, I said, "I think I need a drink from the Sacred River."

We walked the flower-lined path to the river where our spirits were spontaneously strengthened as we knelt and drank. We hugged and then headed for home.

When we reached the park near our homes, we could hear children at play. Four children spotted us and ran excitedly our way.

"So, how are my little girls?" Rita asked hugging Holly and Hailly.

Daniel and Sara gave me hugs and wanted to know all the news from earth.

Rita walked her girls to their homes while I sat on the

grass with Daniel and Sara trying to answer their questions.

"Did you see Satan?" Daniel asked. Sara coiled back when he said the name.

"No, I didn't," I told him. "I hope I never do."

"I'm not afraid of him!" Daniel returned.

"Well, I certainly don't want to see him," Sara said dramatically, her eyes huge. "The Father took his beauty away and he looks very scary!"

"Neither of you should be afraid of Satan," I said. "He can't hurt you."

Sara got up and put her hands on her hips, "Well, why do you suppose those people on earth are so afraid of him?"

"They don't know Jesus, that's why," Daniel mocked her with his hands on his hips.

"Well, they know Him," I corrected Daniel, "but they don't trust Him. It's Rita's and my mission to help the singles in her group trust Jesus and the Father."

Sara sat beside me again and I hugged her and Daniel. Sara looked up at me. "Would you help me with a flower wreath I'm making for a lady who just arrived in heaven?"

New arrivals had become very scarce in heaven and everyone enjoyed welcoming them.

Daniel jumped to his feet. "I want to help too."

"We'll both help you," I said.

Daniel ran to pick some flowers. When he returned, we sat on the grass and wove the flowers together to make a beautiful crown. We worked while listening to magnificent angels' voices singing with the accompaniment of a rehearsing orchestra.

"Heaven is indescribable!" I sighed.

Sara placed the flower wreath on my head and hugged me

Chapter 52 -- Time of Rebellion

The Golden Sea is never muddy or murky; its water is purer than any imaginable on earth. Beautiful underwater flowers bloom in many areas of the soft, scintillating, golden sand on its vast floor.

As I floated in the pristine water, I communed with the Father. "Your peace is greater than any treasure, Father. I know I couldn't be strong during this time without Your peace filling my heart. Thank You."

A wave of the Holy Spirit swept over me. The Father cradled me as though I were a newborn babe in the arms of a proud papa.

"Thou art pure and holy!" I said."

A shaft of light from the Mount of Worship encompassed me and beyond the realms of thought, feeling or emotion I dwelt with the Father for a time. I came back to the reality of heaven when someone bumped into me.

"Sorry," Elaine said, "I wasn't minding where I was floating."

"It's okay. The Holy Spirit told me it's almost time to head for earth, anyway."

"This is the only time I'm tempted to disobey the Father," she said, "when He tells me to get out of the sea. If I still had my earthly body and my sinful nature, I'd be wrinkled as a prune." She laughed.

"I don't think you would really want to disobey the Father under this anointing power." I feigned a look of horror.

"I never thought of that!" The fear of God came over her and she swam quickly toward shore. I laughed at her.

When we reached shore the Holy Spirit immediately transported us to the place of entry.

"I still can't get used to this instant transportation," Elaine said. "Where are we off to, anyway?"

"To visit Gretchen and Nancy."

"Oh! I love ministering to them." She accented her words

with a dance step.

I noticed our guardian angels approaching. "We really appreciate your help," I called out to them. "It would take us forever to get to our mission without it."

Alluding to the powerful demonic forces in the air over earth, one of them said, "I don't think you would make it at all." He added after a pause, "If you did, the reason for your going would no longer exist." The other angel laughed; then they both laughed. Elaine and I just looked at each other.

"Maybe Martha would understand their humor," I thought.

One angel led us while the other followed and we arrived on earth having experienced no opposition. The angels left us as soon as we were secured at our destination.

"Do you suppose they tell us those things to scare us?" Elaine asked.

"No. My guardian angel once had to fight several demons while escorting me to my mission post. You've never come across the enemy on any of your missions?"

"I saw some a few times, but we always had so many angels with us that they didn't dare bother us."

Elaine walked to the door of the home and knocked. Nancy opened the door and invited us in. She had grown to be a beautiful woman and had a wonderful Christian husband. Gretchen lived with them.

Nancy looked relieved to see us. "I'm so glad you're here! Mom is in a tizzy."

We were dismayed to see Gretchen vivid with anger. She muttered something unintelligible while waving a piece of paper at us. "That rebel had the nerve to give this to me!" She thrust it at us. "It's a sacrilege! After all Jesus has done for us!" She sat down, covered her face with her hands and wept.

"Mom," Nancy said, sitting down next to her and putting her arm around her, "this won't help anyone,"

Elaine picked up the paper and read it out loud: *A time for freedom! Freedom to think for ourselves! Freedom to do*

what we know is best for ourselves, and for our country!
Freedom from the strongholds of Christian principles! Free-
dom from the rule of Jesus Christ! I listened in disbelief.

"This is truly a time of darkness!" Nancy said despondently.

We all jumped when Camelia and Alice flew in through the doorway. Alice landed on Nancy's head and Camelia on Gretchen's.

"You brought your angel birds!" Nancy brightened. She put a finger up so Alice could light on it. Gretchen did the same with Camelia. Her spirit seemed to lighten as well.

"It's so good to see you, Camelia," Gretchen said.

Nancy told Alice, "You're even prettier than I remembered." Alice looked embarrassed.

Elaine looked outside to see if anyone had followed the birds. When she couldn't see anyone, she told Nancy and Gretchen that Camelia and Alice must have come with someone else because they hadn't traveled with us.

Her comment agitated Camelia. She squawked loudly and jumped up and down flapping her wings in protest. Then, like a heat-seeking missile, she flew zigzagging maneuvers all around the room, Alice joined her. The two skillfully dodged furniture, plants, us and each other while we watched with gaping mouths. When finished, they lighted again on Gretchen's and Nancy's hands, their little breasts heaving rapidly while waiting for our comments.

"That was really something!" Gretchen exclaimed.

Camelia looked at me and I realized I needed to interpret what they had done. "Camelia and Alice told us that the Father let them come on their own. They showed us how they are able to elude demons." Camelia and Alice confirmed with nods.

"You are so brave!" Nancy lauded Alice, petting her head.

Gretchen laughed approvingly and kissed Camelia's head. Camelia returned a kiss to her cheek. "I love you," Gretchen said sweetly. Camelia responded with a song while hopping on one leg.

Elaine and I had seated ourselves while all this was going on.

"Gretchen and Nancy,"—Elaine paused to see if they were listening—"you need to be like these birds. Share your joy and your love for Jesus with others during this time. This rebellion is indeed a time of sorrow, but you must give all your sorrow, your anger and your fear to the Father. You mustn't hold in your hearts anything that could prevent Jesus' Spirit from ministering to others through you."

Looking back at the bird on her hand, Nancy smiled and said, "I may never fly as fast as you, Alice, but I can be as free as you in my spirit."

"True freedom!" Elaine affirmed. Whenever she felt an anointing, she had to move. Suggesting that we take a stroll through the garden, she eagerly helped me to my feet.

"Great, let's go!" Gretchen said, pleased at the chance to show off her garden. Camelia and Alice flew like bullets through the open doorway to the top of a flowering tree and began to sing joyfully.

"You can't ever say the 'G' word," I whispered to Gretchen on our way outside. "Whenever someone says g.o., these birds disappear." She laughed.

When we reached the garden, I addressed her anger: "Jesus will be victorious; you do know that, don't you?"

Gretchen faced me. "Yes, I know that. It's just that I also know this rebellion hurts Jesus."

Remembering the tear in Jesus' eye when He rode out of heaven to the battle after the tribulation period, and His earlier tears over Jerusalem, I consoled her, saying, "I understand," and hugged her. "We shall overcome," I told her—"just as Jesus overcame the horror of the cross because of the joy awaiting Him."

Elaine sang: "We shall overcome! We shall overcome!"

The rest of us joined in, marching around the garden.

Chapter 53 -- The Approaching Battle

A final battle. The Father Himself would put an end to the forces of evil. It was about to become a historical fact. Satan and his followers would be thrown into the lake of fire and all the unsaved souls, from the time of Adam to the present, would stand before the Great White Throne for judgment. Punishment would be their lot.

Jesus' followers would enter heaven to bask in the glory of the Father. The citizens of heaven were preparing for a major population explosion.

"Do you think Bill would want more windows on this side of the house?" Daryl asked Dad. They were helping carpenters build my brother's home.

"Yes, he'd enjoy a good view of the lake," Dad said while holding a form for Charles to nail.

"I could put a light switch on this wall," Daryl considered. "Just as a memorabilia item." He had been an electrician on earth and had crafted some nostalgic electrical devices in heaven. He produced a switch from a brown bag.

Dad watched him to see if he was serious. Daryl cut out a hole and installed the electrical piece in a finished wall. Dad grinned.

Charles looked at the switch and said, "It's never dark in heaven, so do you suppose he'll ever think to use it?"

Now Daryl observed Charles to see if he was serious. He couldn't tell, so he just laughed and said, "It's not connected." Charles walked over and flipped the switch. The light in the room got much brighter. Three pairs of eyes widened in surprise. Then we heard the Father laughing.

Meanwhile, brother-in-law Bill directed Martha as she carried supplies for the workers.

"A 'beast of burden' is what they call donkeys on earth," Martha told Bill.

"You're not a burden to me; you're my brother—I mean sister."

Martha gave him a curious look, "Is that some sort of 'Bill humor'?"

Bill smiled, "It's an ancient slogan from Boys' Town. More precisely, it was: He's not heavy; he's my brother."

Martha studied him for a moment then chortled to a donkey helping with a neighbor's home: "Bella, come over here. I'd like you to meet my brother, Bill." Bill laughed.

"Just a little 'donkey humor,' Martha told him as she went on ahead of him smirking.

When the men finished the home, they helped my husband and other craftsmen piece together its furnishings.

Mother and Lois made flower arrangements for our arriving siblings. Rita and Lisa designed wall decorations. Char and Jill hung curtains while Elaine and I went from house to house adding finishing touches.

"She likes things open and airy." I draped a shimmering silk curtain to the side of a window.

"Do you think these flowers should be here," Elaine asked holding them near a wall, "or over by this mirror?"

Camelia chirped a response.

"Thank you, Camelia." Elaine placed the flowers by the mirror. She had evidently learned to understand Camelia. She surveyed the room and gave her approval: "It's beautiful!"

I agreed. "I'm getting so excited! They'll all be so surprised when they get here. Earth has been beautiful during Jesus' reign, but nothing compares to the beauty of heaven." I raised my hands in thanksgiving toward the Mount of Worship. "Thank You, Father."

Elaine took a deep breath of air charged with the Holy Spirit's anointing. "It's so glorious!" She looked appreciatively around the room again. "Lori will love this room."

Angelic voices started singing and Elaine danced in praise to the Father. When Camelia saw her twirling around the room, she flew to the center of the floor and flapped her wings while hopping to the music.

It was so much like that first day when Elaine arrived in

heaven. I started weeping with joy. "Oh, Father, I love You so much!" I joined their dance, thrilling at the thought of loved ones who would soon worship with us.

Charles interrupted us, yelling, "You'll have to dance later; an angel just told me that the battle is very close. The enemy has surrounded the camp of God in the holy city."

In the next moment, multiple trumpet blasts came through the windows and reverberated off the walls. The Holy Spirit's anointing fell like heavy snow over heaven. The trumpets sounded again.

"We need to assemble at the Tent of Meeting," Charles relayed to us. "The Apostle John is going to speak." He extended his hand to Elaine and the two of them walked toward the tabernacle. I accompanied them with Camelia on my shoulder.

John looked just like most people would imagine him: tall, dark-brown hair, full beard. His white robe had a waistband made of the same gold cord as his sandals. Love and strength of character shone from his eyes as he leaned over the podium to speak to us.

"Soon, the Father, Who is love personified, will put an end to all ungodliness. Why a just and holy God has put up with Satan and his followers for all these years is beyond my understanding."

We all cheered and shouted, "He is holy and just!"

John shouted, "The rebels of earth have not wanted to glorify God by their lives—now they will glorify Him by their just punishment."

Again, a cheer went up from the citizens of heaven. Many shouted, "Hallelujah!" Someone cried, "Salvation, glory and power belong to our God." Someone else shouted, "True and just are His judgments."

Jesus appeared at the podium next to John and a hush fell over the vast crowd. He embraced John and spoke a few words privately to him. Then, love blazing on His face, He smiled at us comfortingly and said, "Our Father is even more glorified by the holiness and love He showers down upon you, His children." Our hearts melted under His affectionate gaze. I observed that He wore His tallit.

The throng separated as the rulers of earth began to pass through the crowd to approach Jesus. I watched my sons follow along with others after the elders of Israel and the Church. On reaching the open space surrounding Jesus, the rulers fell to their knees and bowed their heads as one.

Peter stood and spoke for the group. "We have been blessed to serve You, honored to have You as our ruler, filled with joy to work with You and know Your presence..."

When Peter finished, the others rose and raised their arms with clenched fists. They declared, "Worthy is the Lamb to receive all praise, honor and glory!"

The sky above Jesus became blinding white and the Father appeared in unapproachable light. Everyone fell facedown while Jesus knelt.

Prostrate, we watched the Father remove the mantle of leadership from Jesus' shoulders and replace it with a mantle of Glory. "Well done, Son. You have been faithful. I am well pleased with You." Tears flowed from Jesus' eyes.

With our faces toward the ground, we extolled our God together: "Our Lord God Almighty reigns!"

When the Father disappeared, we rose to our feet and Jesus said, "I repeat my Father's words to you: Well done my good and faithful friends! In you, I am well pleased!" His words caused a great din.

Jesus rejoiced with us. But then sadness entered His eyes as He raised His hands for silence. "The Father will soon destroy the rebels of earth. Some of you have loved ones in the enemy camp."

Loud weeping broke out in the crowd. I sobbed also.

A mighty wind of the Holy Spirit blew so powerfully across heaven that we were thrown to the ground. The spiritual fire of God's consuming love enveloped us. It seemed to burn for eternity, but it lasted only for the twinkling of an eye. When we stood again, we felt no sorrow—only peace, joy and love.

Jesus smiled lovingly. "When the Great White Throne Judgment is over, we'll celebrate. But for now, go back and prepare for your brothers and sisters who will arrive soon."

We went back to our places of work singing and dancing on our way.

Chapter 54 -- The New Heaven and the New Earth

Death, the final enemy, had been conquered. Our celebration was bigger than any previous event. Multitudes gratefully enjoyed singing, dancing and delicious food. Each citizen of heaven had done missionary work on earth, so we all knew someone among the new arrivals in heaven.

Our festive activities were arrested by jubilant trumpet blasts. Every eye watched the Father destroy earth and its solar system with fire. The Satan-led revolution had rendered earth and its atmosphere unsuitable for the citizens of heaven—much less for a holy God.

Afterward, we watched in awe as Jesus and the Father unveiled the new earth. It had no sun or moon; the Father would be the light, just as He was in heaven.

Trumpets proclaimed the next happening. We stood transfixed as we watched the Father move the City of Our God from heaven to the new earth. It would be called the New Jerusalem.

Gretchen, standing beside me, asked, "Why do they call the New Jerusalem a bride adorned for her husband?"

"Because the bride of Christ—the called, chosen and faithful—will live in the city," I explained. "Elaine is real excited about living there."

"I can understand why," Gretchen said. "It's so majestic and beautiful! Look at all the precious stones in its foundation!"

"Its transparent jasper walls must be over a thousand miles high!" Nancy marveled. "But I don't see any temple."

"No," I said. "There isn't a temple; the Lord is in the city. The thrones of the Father and Jesus are there as well, plus the thrones of the twelve sons of Israel and the twelve apostles of the Lord."

Nancy shielded her eyes from the light of the Father reflecting off the golden streets.

"Look! There's the Sacred River!" Gretchen pointed. "It's flowing from the Throne Room."

"Will you live in the New Jerusalem?" Nancy asked me.

"Yes, but I'll keep my home in heaven as well. My missions will keep me traveling between heaven and the new earth. Jesus and the Father will always be present in both, but the angels will, for the most part, reside in heaven.

"It's so overwhelming!" Gretchen sighed. "I keep wondering why I found it so difficult to serve Jesus before His reign. I remember having only a vague idea of what heaven would be like. All I knew for sure was that I wanted to be where He was." I understood her completely and hugged her.

Jesus had been discretely greeting celebrants and was now approaching us. He lovingly embraced Gretchen and then Nancy. "Welcome to heaven."

Glancing at me, He said, "We are so glad you're here." I had heard Him speak those words to others; yet, each time He said them to me my heart melted.

Gretchen and Nancy were so overcome by His presence that they couldn't speak. They cried softly as He held them both in His arms.

After a moment He stood back and asked them, "Have you seen the new sector of heaven where the City of Our God used to be?"

They shook their heads.

He turned to me. "Why don't you take your sisters and show it to them."

I stammered, "I haven't seen it either. Did the Father just create it?"

His eyes twinkled. "Yes, We just finished it."

"Thank You, Jesus!" I grabbed Nancy's and Gretchen's hands and shouted "Let's go!" as if I were leading a wagon train westward.

Camelia perched on my shoulder. "You must have been within hearing range," I said. "I gather you would like to join us." She did her little dance.

Gretchen and Nancy looked at Jesus as though they thought He would come along.

"I have other brothers and sisters to welcome," He told them. "I will see you both again soon."

As we started out for the newly created sector of heaven, we saw Elaine leading Martha our way.

"The Father told us where you are going," Elaine said excitedly when they reached us. "May we walk with you?"

Gretchen and Nancy were both still speechless and responded with hugs. Gretchen kept her arms around Martha's neck for a long time. Elaine gave me an understanding look.

Martha then walked on ahead and started singing:

> *Oh the circle won't be broken,*
> *Bye and bye Lord, bye and bye....*

The rest of us joined in. After the final stanza, the Father said, "I have given each of you the desires of your heart."

Camelia chirped, "Amen."

Yes, I remember so clearly my arrival in heaven. It

seems like just yesterday. And already I'm about to enter into a glory that no eye has seen, no ear has heard, nor mind has comprehended.

Epilogue

When a believer's earthly mission is completed, he or she begins a new mission in heaven. Obedience is the key. It is required of all who would reign with Jesus.

Scripture instructs us to think about those things that are above—whatever is true, noble, right, pure, lovely, admirable, excellent or praiseworthy.

As the world grows colder with sin and lawlessness, individuals may be tempted to leave this world for a better one by ending their life. God's Word tells us that ending one's life unnaturally and prematurely is an act void of faith in God. And without faith in Him it is impossible to please Him. Those displeasing in His sight will not enter His Kingdom. Trust in God; He will not fail you. He will give you the help you need to obey Him.